John Wayne:
A Novel

Happy ♡
♡ Birthday
Dad ♡
I Love you ♡
—Brittany
☺

2023

JOHN WAYNE: A NOVEL

DAN BARDEN

ANCHOR BOOKS
DOUBLEDAY
NEW YORK LONDON TORONTO
SYDNEY AUCKLAND

AN ANCHOR BOOK
PUBLISHED BY DOUBLEDAY
a division of Bantam Doubleday Dell
Publishing Group, Inc.
1540 Broadway, New York, New York 10036

John Wayne: A Novel was originally published in
hardcover by Doubleday in 1997. The Anchor
Books edition is published by arrangement with
Doubleday.

This novel is a work of historical fiction. Names,
characters, places, and incidents relating to
nonhistorical figures are either the product of the
author's imagination or are used fictitiously. Any
resemblance of such nonhistorical incidents, places,
or figures to actual events or locales or persons,
living or dead, is entirely coincidental.

"Do You Know the Way to San Jose?" Lyric by Hal
David. Music by Burt Bacharach. Copyright © 1967
(Renewed) Casa David and New Hidden Valley
Music. International Copyright Secured. All Rights
Reserved.

Book design by Jennifer Ann Daddio
Frontispiece courtesy of Bettman Archive

The Library of Congress has cataloged the
hardcover edition of this book as follows:
Barden, Dan, 1960–
John Wayne : a novel / by Dan Barden.
p.   cm.
1. Wayne, John, 1907–1979—Fiction.
I. Title.
PS3552.A6144J6   1997
813'.54—dc21   96-47273
CIP

ISBN 0-385-48710-X

Printed in the United States of America

First Anchor Books Edition: October 1998

1 3 5 7 9 10 8 6 4 2

This is a house I built for my mother

ACKNOWLEDGMENTS

Writing is *not* a lonely business. I'm grateful for the love, support, and good works of: Dr. Tom Sholseth and Jan Sholseth, Liz Szabla, Charles Flowers, my editor Pat Mulcahy, Denell Downum, Rick Moody, Suzanne Jackson, James Linville, Adrienne Miller, Garry and Natalie Wills, Margaret Dawe, Christopher Barden, Tom and Libya Clancy, Thomas Mallon, Breon Dunigan and Bob Bailey, Tom Feigelson, Nicole Gregory, Augie Hasho, Lynn Holst, Brianne Leary, Colleen Keegan, Jeffrey Hogrefe, Wendy Hull, Lori Grant, Keith Klein and Becky Brown, Faith Meade, Sarah Price and Dan Courtenay, Karen Rinaldi, Barbara Jones and Steven Rinehart, Lillian Barden and Gordon Rieger, Juan Martinez, Anastasia Simone, Eleanor Bowie, Susan Schorr, Charles Silver, Lee Smith, Kristoffer Jacobson, Peter Stitt, Peter Stine, S. Kirk Walsh, Keith Dunlap, Sally Wofford Girand, Kathryn Gravdal, the memory of Tom Vericker . . .

and for the love and tender mercies of my supervising angels: Mary-Beth Hughes, Alice Barden, and my agent Lydia Wills.

CONTENTS

When I started, I knew I was no actor and I

went to work on this Wayne thing.

It was as deliberate and studied a projection

as you'll ever see.

—John Wayne

PROLOGUE

1923

DUKE WANTED IT TO BE A STORY ABOUT WHITE SLAVERY. AS HIS FATHER'S TRUCK APPROACHED, HE TRIED TO IMAGINE GIRLS IN LOCKED, WINDOWLESS ROOMS WHOSE ONLY ESCAPE WAS WHAT THEY COULD SEE THROUGH A KEYHOLE. HIS FATHER SLOWED DOWN, BUT DUKE SIGNALED HIM TO KEEP MOVING SO THAT HE COULD DO A DOUGLAS FAIR-BANKS INTO THE BACK OF the truck. Clyde Morrison watched his son vault the side panel, and he picked up speed once he could see that Duke was settled in the back.

No, Duke thought, I don't like a story that starts in a locked room. It lacked the potential for fistfights. It was his experience that fistfights occurred out of doors unless they were between a man and his wife. No locked rooms.

Duke dragged a sack of sand against the cab, where his father's head bounced along with the truck. He leaned back to watch the disconnected sky pass above him. Eucalyptus trees rushed by. He'd been running through the Verdugo Hills in preparation for football season, and the only thing he liked about road-work was when it was over.

It might be better if it were a cabin on the edge of a wilderness, the kind of place that was good for stories. It could be about a woman who had *escaped* from white slavery. She'd met a man who didn't care about her past, and now they lived in a wilderness cabin. When trouble came, the brave family would meet it in the open. The wife would stand behind her husband. The husband would brandish a rifle. The intruders—the same men who had locked her in the windowless room—would be defeated from the height of a hill after a fierce and bloody battle in which maybe even the husband was wounded. But the intruders would never dare return. No, better than that—they'd all be dead.

When they stopped at the railroad tracks for a southbound train, Duke leapt from the truckbed and got into the cab beside his father. Duke loved his father—that was what all his daydreams were ultimately about.

"Decided to move up with the grown-ups?"

"Yes, sir."

"What were you dreaming about back there?"

"I don't think you want to know."

"Thinking about a girl at school?"

"Something like that."

As the train passed them—a yellow-and-red Southern Pacific, big as a dinosaur—Clyde smiled and returned his attention to the road.

"Dad?"

"Yeah."

"She was wrong last night. Everything she said was wrong."

"I don't know what you're talking about, son."

"She blamed you for the farm not working out, and she made it sound like the drugstore was a bad idea, too. It made me mad."

"Have you spoken to her about this?"

"No."

"Does she know you were listening?"

"No."

"Good. Keep it that way. There's no sense in her hating both of us."

"I think it's too late for that," Duke said.

Clyde opened his mouth to speak, but nothing came out. Absurdly enough, she *did* hate both of them.

"I didn't mean that," Duke said. "I'm sorry."

"Well, when you get married, maybe you'll be smarter than I was."

Sometimes Duke wanted to be more like his father, but this wasn't one of those times. There was a flaw in Clyde's thinking, and when Duke found it, the whole structure of his father's personality would fall like an old shack in the wind. Duke knew where the problem started, though—it started with his father's tremendous ability to forgive: forgive his wife, forgive his parents, forgive his bad lungs, forgive this crowded town which had brought him no less trouble than Iowa or Lancaster—the places they had lived before.

He watched his father drive toward Glendale, and he remembered the times when Clyde had become another kind of man. When his father drank too much—a seasonal occurrence, like rain or windstorms—he found a part of himself that was entirely bitter, as bitter as his wife had ever been. That was when he broke the furniture and threatened her and she shook with fear. That was when he blamed her as much as she blamed him. That was when Duke had to stand between them. He could count on one hand the times this had happened.

"You know what your coach told me this morning?" Clyde asked.

"No, what?"

"He said, 'There's nothing ailing Glendale football that five more Duke Morrisons wouldn't cure.' "

Duke adored his father, but lately he'd been disturbed by the differences between them—which Clyde often brought to his attention. At sixteen, Duke was already the darling of the local papers, a young man whom mothers wanted for their daughters, a young man who made older men ashamed of their indolence. Clyde, on the other hand, was a man with a respiratory disease who ran a pharmacy owned by the bank.

When they arrived downtown, Clyde asked Duke to unload the sand near the back of the drugstore. Why he needed sand, Duke didn't know and didn't care. He'd watched his feelings turn this way before, and it was never pleasant. As Clyde's head disappeared into the darkness of the pharmacy, Duke couldn't help thinking that he'd been cheated, that this wasn't the kind of father he deserved. The more he thought this way, the more ashamed of himself he became.

His father's drugstore, near the corner of Harmony and Vasquez, was a peaceful place that attracted the older men and the younger women. Clyde teased Duke that the girls only came around to catch a glimpse of him, but Duke knew it had more to do with Clyde. Clyde understood the trick of making young girls feel attractive but never threatened.

As Duke followed his father through the back of the store, he remembered one girl whom Clyde particularly enjoyed cheering up. Her name was Maria, and even Duke recognized that she didn't belong in Glendale. She was a pretty girl, but not pretty in the way a small town valued. She was also a smart girl. Clyde loved her, Duke imagined, because she was the daughter he would have liked to have had.

When they turned on all the lights, Maria was standing outside the front door. Duke felt as though he had conjured her from the air. It was the middle of Sunday afternoon, but the tinted shades made it feel like dusky evening, and Maria's face, just beyond the darkened window, was changed from how Duke remembered it. The lines of awkwardness were gone and she was beautiful like a movie actress or a pinup girl. Duke hurried toward the door to let her in.

Clyde shouted from the back of the room, "Hello, beautiful girl!" and Maria blinked to be so suddenly confronted by his attention. She shook Duke's hand and walked past him toward his father. Most of Maria's errands to the drugstore were invented, but Clyde would never challenge her. Duke's mother was convinced that Clyde's business would thrive without this kind of frivolity, but Duke recognized that this kind of frivolity *was* his father's business. There were times when Duke wanted to slap his mother, the depth of her misunderstanding was so great.

Maria assembled fifty cents' worth of cosmetics and candy and offered them to the bag that Clyde held out for her.

"Okay, sweetheart. Will there be anything else?"

"No, Mr. Morrison. I just wanted to pick up a few things. Thanks for opening the store."

"What do you hear about my son Duke? Is he a big heart-breaker at the high school?"

Maria turned toward the door where Duke was still linger-ing, but she stopped herself. She wouldn't look at him. "I know a lot of girls that like him," she said.

Clyde smiled and threw a few extra pieces of candy into her bag. "I think you're breaking a few hearts yourself," he said.

Duke smiled. If he stood there long enough, he would no longer be ashamed of his father. He knew that by long experience. He watched Maria—she wore a summer dress, she was so much smaller than he was—and he imagined his hand sliding up her dress, over her ass and up her back, to where he could turn her around like a puppet and kiss her the way he'd always wanted to kiss a girl. Not the little pecks of the cheerleaders after a football game, but a deep exchange of everything that was inside them. His father looked at him over Maria's head, and Duke could feel the erection starting to fill his pants.

"Duke?"

"Yes, sir."

"Why don't you drive Maria home and get me another bag of sand on your way past the quarry?"

"Sir?"

"I know that doesn't make sense. I could have picked it up earlier, but it didn't occur to me. I've got about a half hour's work to do here, so that'll keep you busy for just the right amount of time."

Duke didn't mind driving Maria home. The sand bothered him, though. It was the kind of thing that drove Duke's mother crazy. Indecision. Forgetfulness. Two trips when one would do. Typically, the waste was wrapped in a kindness that made it hard to criticize him.

Duke put her bicycle in the back of the truck. Maria was quiet for the first mile, but she answered easily when he asked her a question. She watched the neighborhoods pass until Duke asked her another question. "What does your father do, again?"

"He was a doctor, but now he's retired."

"Why did he retire?"

"He made a lot of money."

Maria smiled. Duke rolled down the window and set his arm on the door, just like Clyde.

"What does he do now?"

"He reads books and rides horses. He hunts and fishes."

"Do you ride horses?"

"I don't like horses much, but I ride them because it makes my father happy. He thinks it's something everyone should do for their health. I like cars better. I don't feel sorry for a car because I'm sitting on its back."

"Well, maybe you *should* feel sorry for it," Duke said. "There's been a whole lot more on the back of this truck than any horse ever carried."

"But a truck doesn't have a soul," Maria said. "So I'm not going to have to look into its big eyes when I meet it in heaven and it asks me why I spent so much of my life sitting on it."

Duke laughed. She had a funny way of looking at things, and she was much prettier than he'd imagined. She had a strong, straight nose and full lips. Her dark eyes brightened when Duke asked her a question.

When they reached her address, the gravel driveway was lined with flagstones. The building itself was alone on a long, shallow hillside, a hacienda that might have been older than the state of California. A huge porch covered two sides, and from where he sat, Duke couldn't guess how big the house itself was. It had the cheerfully decaying surface of a colonial building.

"This is my house," Maria said. "It doesn't look like anyone else's house, does it?"

It hadn't occurred to him that she might be Spanish. The house itself was no reason to think that, but he thought it anyway.

"Are you Catholic?"

"Yes," she said. "Are you?"

"No."

Duke had nothing more to say. He was awed by her home, but unwilling to talk about it. He watched it through the windshield. With all those flat, cool surfaces, it was like a cloud sitting on the ground.

"Would you like to see?"

"Yeah."

They crossed the crunching gravel toward the front door, which was black with red trim. He didn't know why he was following her into the house. Every step was closer to a darkness he couldn't identify, but now keenly felt in Maria's presence. It was like the darkness of regretting his parents, but more painful.

"You don't have any brothers and sisters?" Duke asked.

"No, I don't."

The main room—he didn't know what to call it, a living room? an entry hall?—was more masculine than any room he'd ever been in. Every seat was covered in leather and framed in dark wood. The pictures on the walls were scenes of horses and hunting. Even the flowers, which brought a welcome brightness to the table and mantelpiece, were not the flowers a woman would have chosen. The colors were hard and strong and deliberate.

"Where's your mother?" Duke asked.

"She died when I was a little girl."

"I'm sorry." Duke watched her for signs of her mother's absence. Her eyes were dark and wide. Her lips settled into a thin frown.

"She lived in New York for a long time," Maria said.

Duke followed Maria through the house. As alien as it first seemed to him—all the wood and leather and nowhere a woman's touch—he soon realized that it was exactly the kind of house he wanted. If he had dreamed this place, he couldn't have made it any better.

His imagination of Maria deepened. She was a child who'd probably never had a mother, and that was a freedom he could feel. He could see it in the way her shoulders lifted her dress and the way her arms fell simply away from her shoulders. Of course, she was Spanish. She had the dark eyes of the earliest settlers. She had the softness of a culture that put men above everything.

"I want to ask about your mother. Is it all right to ask about your mother?"

"I don't think you want to know."

"Maybe I do."

"Why?"

"What happened to her? Why did she go away?"

"My mother didn't like it here. She pretended to like it because it made my father happy."

"But what happened?"

"One night, she got really mad at me because I had just

9

learned how to fill the tub and I let it overflow—by accident. She slapped me a couple of times. I think she was afraid of what would happen to the house, and I think she would have stopped, but Dad grabbed her and tried to hold her down. She went wild after that. She broke his nose. She never calmed down."

"Why did she go to New York?"

"My dad put her in a sanitarium there. He said it was the best in the world."

"You make it sound like it wasn't."

"I don't know," Maria said. "That was where she died. It couldn't have been *that* good." She turned to face the fireplace. "Dad said that it was heart disease, that it wasn't anyone's fault."

Because Maria wasn't crying, Duke felt as though he might cry himself. As he watched her try to shake off her emotions, he thought about the houses he'd grown up in. They were comfortable, but filled with humiliation. His parents would fight over money, and sometimes his mother would ask for Duke's paper route earnings right in front of Clyde. Why did she have to do that? Duke had prayed Clyde would hit her, just hard enough to stop her from destroying everything Duke loved about his family.

Maria's house didn't have a mother, and Maria's sadness would have been Duke's joy. As much as he wanted to grieve for her, the house still made him happy. The things that surrounded him were the things he would want for the rest of his life. He put his hand on Maria's shoulder and gently turned her around.

"I want to kiss you," Duke said.

Her eyes brightened, but she didn't speak.

"Don't you want that?" he asked.

"I did a few minutes ago."

"Did I do something wrong?"

"No, you've been the best gentleman. It's just, it's strange being here together. It feels too much like his house. I feel like he's watching us."

"It's a really nice house," Duke said. "I liked it right away."

"There's never anyone here but my father and I. Don't you think that's kind of sad?"

"I think that's very sad."

She leaned toward him and he held her. "Big houses shouldn't be for just a few people," she said. "They should be for lots of people. With a big house like this, I think you should have lots of children and lots of friends."

"I think you're right."

Duke looked around again, and it seemed even more like his home. The only things he'd change were what Maria wanted to change. If this were really his house, it would be filled with pictures of the large family that lived here. The noise of children would be everywhere. The smell of cooking would always be announcing the next meal. He would fill the tables with *bright* flowers.

"Why don't you just pretend it's your house," Duke said. "That'll make it easier, won't it?"

He thought he'd seen everything there was, but sitting by itself on a small wooden table beside the telephone stand was a wedding picture, smothered by an ornate gilt frame.

"Is that your mother?"

"Yes." Maria smiled. "Isn't it a pretty picture?" Maria picked it up and offered it to Duke.

She was a strong-featured girl, not so different from Maria, but more beautiful in the conventional terms that a camera could understand. She was wearing her wedding gown, and she was three or four years older than Maria was now.

"She must have been beautiful," Duke said.

"She was."

"You never visited her in New York?"

"We visited her sometimes. I think he didn't want me to visit her too much."

Duke bent down to kiss Maria. He held her carefully between his hands.

Kissing her, Duke could feel the life he was about to begin. He would live in big houses filled with lovely people. He wasn't going to become his father because he would never choose a woman like his mother. Suddenly, that part had become very simple. But he would still lose something he'd always thought he needed. He tried to suppress this understanding, but it just became more powerful. He could enjoy kissing Maria for the rest of his life—he *did* enjoy kissing her—and he would never know why his mother hated him so much.

He stood back from Maria's face. There were many lifetimes there. The life she had lived and the life she had yet to live, her mother's life and her father's life. Duke's life, too. He wanted to believe that she wasn't going to get any older, that he could protect her from all harm, but what he saw instead was the kind of mother she might become: vicious, destructive, drunk, insane, dead. There were too many possibilities.

His own mother's face began to crowd his imagination. She hadn't always been a bitch. Even now, she could be kind, and there were days when she made him proud. When it came down to it, Duke was more like Molly Morrison than he'd ever been like Clyde. Duke had watched her raise her family from Iowa to Glendale, but she couldn't do it without the help of her men, and that fact angered her beyond her ability to control herself. Duke knew how she felt. He wanted to be free of his family as much as she did. After a while, her face had been destroyed by her anger. She wasn't a beautiful woman anymore. She hadn't been a beautiful woman for a long time.

Maria was getting frightened. She wasn't an experienced girl, and the handsomest boy at Glendale High just continued to stare at her.

"Duke, what's wrong?"

"Nothing."

"Something's wrong."

Duke watched her eyes. Her eyes were perfect like her mother's eyes, dark but radiant. She didn't know him at all, but she knew him better than anyone in the world. She was the first person he'd met in this new life. He held her hand and kissed her again, but he couldn't feel the passion he'd felt a moment earlier.

"What were you thinking about? Why'd you stop kissing me?"

"My mother was so beautiful."

"What do you mean?"

"I was thinking about how beautiful your mother was, and it reminded me of my mother, the way she used to be."

Maria held his hand tightly. Duke gave her a thin smile and narrowed his eyes. He wanted her and he hated himself for wanting her. But in spite of everything, he tried to be adequate to what she felt for him. "I mean, you're beautiful, too. You're *so* beautiful. I'm sorry your mother's gone, though."

He took both her hands and placed them between his own hands. He extended his fingers as though his tenderness were compounded by strength. He watched himself, becoming certain as the gesture closed around her that it was exactly right. Deep inside, though, he was breaking like glass.

Maria's face softened. "We don't talk about her. My dad believes in all that Mexican stuff. *Feo, fuerte, y formal.*"

"I don't know what that means."

"The Mexicans say that a man should be ugly and strong, but have dignity. It means, well, it means that a man shouldn't be too pretty, that he should work hard, and that he should hide his true feelings." Maria smiled at the intensity of Duke's interest. She kissed his big hand. "You're strong and you're dignified, but you're a little too dreamy to be *feo*. Maybe when you're older."

Duke frowned. He narrowed his eyes again, watching to see how she would react.

"You should probably go now. My dad's going to be back, and I don't think you're quite *feo* enough for him, either."

He put his arm under her shoulder blade and gently pulled her forward. He kissed her hard on the lips without opening his mouth.

Outside, in the short time they had talked, the sky had deepened. What had been hazy blue was now hard amber. He hadn't seen a sky like this in a long time. It was as though all the elements of earth and air had conspired to make a sheen so impenetrable that no human thought could get beyond it.

"What kind of doctor was your father?" Duke asked.

"Mostly horses and large mammals."

"He was a vet? I thought you said he was a doctor?"

"I'm sorry. That's what he calls himself—a doctor. For a while, he was a rancher, too."

"My father was a farmer," Duke said.

"Really?"

"For a little while."

Before his parents moved to Glendale, they had lived in Lancaster, beyond the San Gabriel Mountains in the Mojave Desert. His father had tried to become a farmer, but as hard as he worked, he couldn't make the land profitable. In the desert, the sky was often impenetrable, even when it was clear blue and saturated with light. Duke had a horse then. The horse had been skinny because of a disease, but no one had known except his family. As Duke drove away from the hacienda—Maria waved after him—he tried to imagine how that must have looked to the neighbors. His father had been a foolish farmer, and his mother had been mean even then. The neighbors must have thought they were starving the animal. He wished he knew why no one had said anything. It would have been so simple to ask, but no one ever had.

As he drove back toward the quarry, Duke rehearsed the trip home. He would get another bag of sand, return to the drugstore, and put it wherever his father wanted. He still didn't know what Clyde intended to make with all that goddamn sand, but he felt prepared to become the best version of Clyde's son that he could imagine. Maybe they would make something good together.

JOHN WAYNE'S

CHRISTMAS

PARTY

1971

At one distant point in her life, it seemed as if a whole team of attractive young Jewish men were courting Lillian Barden. She never told her mother until it became too important *NOT* to tell her mother. And that was the end of them, whoever the hell they were. Once she told her mother, that was the end of the Jewish boys.

Why was Lillian thinking about this on the drive to Newport Beach? *Oh, she knew what it was.* When they came over the top of Newport Boulevard and could see the ocean for the first time, it reminded her of the way Manhattan could sometimes surprise her when she returned to it from the Bronx. When she was a teenager, she would think, Oh my God, I'm really going back to New York City. Even though she was born there, she had grown up in the Bronx, and the fact of Manhattan could make her happy to her heart's deep core. And now, with her husband Frank driving them toward the Pacific Ocean, toward Newport Beach beside the Pacific Ocean, she thought, Oh my God, I'm really going to John Wayne's Christmas party.

Phil and Arlene Szabla were in the backseat counting their blessings. Lillian turned and lifted her arm over the seat back to give them encouragement, although she wasn't much engaged with the conversation. To a greater or lesser degree, everyone in the car was a star-struck teenager willing themselves to become the appropriate adult who would be worthy of this great honor.

"Tell me about the boat again," Phil said. He was the kind of midwestern man California was full of. With a well cared-for mustache and circumspect manners, he made corny jokes out of anything that happened to him. "Maybe they'll take me on the crew."

"A ship," Frank corrected him. "It's practically a ship."

Arlene made a noise like a puppy, a mewing bark. Lillian smiled and thought about Jewish boys who might now be her husband. She *had* to marry a Catholic; she couldn't marry a Jew. Why was she thinking about this on the night that everyone in the car agreed was the night of Frank's triumph? She didn't even know any Jewish men in California.

Duke Wayne lived at the end of Bayshore Drive, just a few minutes off Pacific Coast Highway. She had visited his house before because Frank had remodeled it. The details of its reconstruction and enhancement had obsessed him for more than a year, and Lillian couldn't help but share his obsession, as she shared his obsession with most houses he worked on.

Apropos of nothing that had been said in the car up to that point, Arlene mentioned that she was making a list of the celebrities she would *like* to see at the party but didn't think she would see at the party. Arlene was a twitchy young woman who looked as though she would never be more comfortable than at her own kitchen table, chain-smoking cigarettes and drinking coffee and talking her way through her children's lives. Recently, she and Phil had moved to Lompoc, a town northwest of Santa Barbara that was as near to nowhere as Lillian had ever been.

Frank, who until now had been driving with the inevitable concentration of a chauffeur, fell back for a moment from his mission and seemed to take offense at the suggestion that there could be *anything* wrong with John Wayne's Christmas party. Actually, for a moment there, he demonstrated a very John Wayne–like bewilderment. His brow creased as his eyes got small and sad and terrifically focused. His mouth closed into a thin, severe line. Lillian saw his thoughts. She leaned back toward Arlene.

"Now, who *wouldn't* be there tonight, Arlene?" She spoke the way she might speak to her children, calculating how to cajole them into good sense.

"Elvis Presley, first of all. I don't think Elvis Presley's going to be there. David Brinkley. Ricky Nelson. Neil Armstrong . . . ." Frank turned to offer a severe face into the backseat. Arlene continued more quickly, ". . . Gore Vidal. Hugh Hefner. Roman Polanski."

"That's an odd list of names," Lillian said. "What makes you think they won't be there?"

Phil, obviously straining to support Lillian's position, said, "Ricky Nelson was in a movie with John Wayne, and Elvis has made more than a few Westerns."

"Only three," Arlene corrected him, *"Charro!* and *Love Me Tender* and *Flaming Star*. I don't want to argue about that. Besides, I'm not trying to make a point that these people won't be there. I just *feel* like they won't be there. Anyway, I think my heart would just burst if I started concentrating on who I think *will* be there. Just thinking about meeting John Wayne himself is enough to kill me."

For some reason, that put the smile back on Frank's face and he continued to drive with dignity and focus. Lillian watched this transition with the curiosity of a scientist. What was it exactly that made this man happy?

After a moment of contented silence, Frank began to explain what would happen to them when they arrived. "We'll give the car to the valet parking fellow, and then we'll walk through the house toward the tent that Duke's set up on the lawn. That's so the party can't be ruined by rain. That's where most of the action is going to be. Once we get settled, I'll show you the work we did on the house. Oh yeah, there's also this business of getting back and forth to the *Wild Goose*. There's gonna be a little ferry, and maybe later, we can go out and take a look at the boat."

"Ship!" Phil corrected with mock sternness.

"You got me," Frank said. "Ship."

Up to a point, the first hour of the evening went just as Frank had predicted. The parking attendant took their blue-black Buick

Electra and stashed it somewhere among the many other cars that lined the drive to Wayne's house. Unaccustomed to surrendering her vehicle, Lillian wondered how they would ever find it again. There was no John Wayne at the door to greet them, but Pilar, his wife, made a very nice impression on Arlene and Phil by kissing Frank on both cheeks and embracing Lillian like the dearest friend. After a few moments of introduction and Pilar's fond compliments to the man who had remodeled her probably already beautiful home, the two couples found themselves somewhere beneath the red-and-white-striped tent that covered the better part of John Wayne's lawn. They had been introduced to yet another couple, but somehow that third couple had drifted away from them toward another end of the tent. The party was just getting started and there were still great spaces between groups of people. Lillian wondered if she should feel slighted by Pilar's efficiency. Frank seemed grateful to spend a moment trying to inhabit his tuxedo. Phil and Arlene were looking to Frank and Lillian for clues as to how they should feel about anything.

"I'm seeing lots of people I think I know but can't put a name to," Arlene whispered to Lillian. "Everyone in that area over there seems like they've got their own TV show."

"They act like it anyway," Lillian said.

"Oh," Arlene said. "We're playing it cool. Is that it?"

"I'm waiting for the real stars to show up," Lillian smiled. She remembered the day a boy had taken her ice skating in Manhattan and she'd seen Lauren Bacall shepherding a flock of children up Fifth Avenue. There had been moments when Lillian wanted her life to have as much reality as Lauren Bacall's, but until tonight she hadn't thought this way for years. John Wayne's house and that phony pumped-up party feeling—her anticipation, like everyone else's, of what this night would bring—were making her think deep thoughts about her ability to shape the universe around her, or maybe just the ten or fifteen inches that surrounded her skinny young woman's body.

Fifteen inches was about how far her husband Frank stood from her. He was trying to look like a man, which wasn't too difficult, but maybe he didn't know that. He was a big, blocky ex-marine just starting to go soft at the edges. He had heroically strong arms and a flattop the barber leveled every other week. He was a sweet but mostly fearful man whom God graced from time to time with the courage for one good idea that made Lillian shudder with excitement for their future together. Although she could see that he hadn't been her best choice, by now they had three children, and she could also see that neither had he been an entirely bad choice. He held his hands together behind his back like a beat cop stretching himself. Frank looked down at the floor and then up at Lillian.

"We're going to go get a drink," he said. "You gals want anything?"

The only movie that had ever meant anything to Lillian was *Ben-Hur*. She dropped from her life for one whole day in 1959 to watch it three times in a row from the same seat in the Ziegfeld Theatre in Manhattan. She was engaged to Frank by then—although she changed her mind every day—and she had a good job at Teachers Insurance Company in the city. She was twenty-two years old. Sometimes still, she fell asleep at night thinking about Stephen Boyd's twisted face as he confronts Charlton Heston for the last time. The villain is dying. The light in his eyes has almost gone out, and the whole world waits to see if this Roman scum has it in his heart to offer some consolation to Judah Ben-Hur, the Jewish prince whose life he has destroyed and who has now, in turn, destroyed him. But there is no mercy. There is no consolation. With his dying breath he reveals to Judah that his mother and sister have become lepers, that Judah's situation, even at the moment of his triumph, is worse than he could possibly have imagined. Now in her mid-thirties, Lillian still remembered the vicious look on Stephen Boyd's face.

But beyond *Ben-Hur,* the movies hadn't been much of a force in her life. The same was probably true of her husband Frank. They saw what everyone else saw. They watched television. It wasn't until Frank started to work for John Wayne that this world opened up for them, that they imagined any mystery or meaning behind the stories up on the screen.

Arlene led Lillian through the larger crowds that now surrounded John Wayne's house. They had taken a ferry to the *Wild Goose* and somehow lost their husbands in the process. A few minutes earlier, John Wayne himself had appeared for a moment through the sliding glass door that connected his house to the patio, but he had an air of business, as though he hadn't yet entered the party. Inspired by John Wayne's brief appearance, Arlene was determined to display goal-oriented behavior. They made their way toward the house as though they knew what they were doing. They had no idea where their husbands were. A path cleared toward the patio, but they hung for a moment in the middle distance, Lillian holding Arlene back from her headlong advance. It seemed to her as though there were too many men who had turned too many faces toward them. The urgency in the men's faces made the women who attended—most of them dressed more beautifully than Arlene and Lillian would have imagined appropriate—suddenly seem like so many grazing beasts.

"Bruce Cabot," Arlene whispered, nodding toward one of

the bright faces calculating their hesitance. Lillian watched herself watched by a tall, slightly overweight, more than middle-aged man whose skin was bronzed past any recognizable flesh tone. He seemed pleased with himself to such an extent that self-congratulation had become a habit which had etched strong lines in his face. He held his drink a little too high, and although he was a handsome older man, there was something foppish in the way he protected his drink from the world, as though he were afraid someone would grab at it from below him.

"I don't know," Lillian said.

"He was in *King Kong*. He's been in a lot of John Wayne movies, too."

Lillian took some pleasure in the fact that she didn't know him, and as she and Arlene talked, the man continued to stare at her long after the other bright faces had turned back toward their drinks and their partners. Lillian looked away from him toward Newport Harbor. Balboa Peninsula looked like a Christmas tree turned over on its side and half-sunk into the ocean. Lights of green and blue and red stretched and shimmered and softened as they reached across the water toward John Wayne's lawn. The air was almost cool, barely suggesting the season. Lillian said, "This is not far from where we live, is it?"

In spite of Lillian's digression, Arlene was still engaged with the party. "I guess he's never been that appealing to me," Arlene said, "but I remember him, which says something in his favor. There are so many people whose names I *wouldn't* remember."

As Lillian returned her attention to the party, she saw Frank floating toward her, his shoulders secured by Bruce Cabot's arm, Phil following close behind. It was as though her inattention had conjured them.

Bruce Cabot's smile was still full of sexual mischief, even up this close, even with his arm around her husband. Or maybe *because* he had his arm around her husband. When Frank introduced them all, the movie star offered big hugs to the two women, which startled Lillian and tickled Arlene. Lillian thought she felt a hand wander below her waist and over her ass. Cabot smelled of booze and stale cigarette smoke and another woman's perfume. There was no telling where he'd been and whose ass he'd been fondling before he got to Lillian's.

"Frank's going to build me a big house, too," Cabot said, lifting his drink. "Bigger than Duke's if I have anything to say about it. Somebody's got to keep these nouveau riche Hollywood assholes in line, and Frank and I are the guys to do it. Phil, too. Right, Phil?"

"Right, Bruce."

"Pardon my bad manners, ladies, I'm just a little exuberant with the party. Sorry to swear."

Lillian realized that nothing was required of her but a nod. A man like Cabot was capable of generating his own conversation. She barely listened as Arlene attempted to join whatever world Cabot belonged to.

"Oh, Bruce, you know you can talk anyway you want around us."

Lillian watched Bruce Cabot's once handsome, now harshly lined face, and she gave herself a moment to consider what was going on around her. The party was filling the way a pool fills with water. The tables, which had looked stark beyond the caterer's attempts to dress them up—large displays of orchids and snapdragons and mums at the center of each, festive cards announcing Pilar and Duke Wayne's pleasure to be having another Christmas party—now began to seem genuinely festive as the different-shaped glasses holding different-colored drinks brought a randomness to each arrangement that reminded Lillian of weddings and the delight that people took in disarray after careful and complete order. It was this moment, too, when she began to see stars whom she *really* recognized—she wouldn't have known Bruce Cabot from a greengrocer. Johnny Weissmuller was on the other side of the room looking old but still massively beautiful. He reminded Lillian of her plain-faced husband. Hugh O'Brian was hugging another man just to the left of her. Jill St. John was speaking loudly to three sharp-faced tuxedos beside John Wayne's pool. Richard Boone was now grazing in the middle distance on a handful of party snacks.

Bruce Cabot asked her if she'd ever been an actress herself. The line had a tired elegance. Years of use must have worn it down into smoothness. She met her husband's eyes and willed him to respond for her—put up a wall against Cabot's flirtation—but Frank seemed anxious to hear her answer.

"No," she said brightly. "I've always been a little too stiff and shy for that. I like to stay at home and read about glamorous lives. I don't think I could ever live one."

"It gets easier after a while." Cabot smiled. "It's like any game. You hit your stride if you play it long enough."

"How long have you been playing it?" she asked. Indeed, Lillian was hitting her stride just now as they spoke. Her husband had nothing to add, and he seemed a little numb but proud of the familiar way she engaged Bruce Cabot. She was even beginning to feel a little proud of herself when a voice from behind the three men—Phil, Frank, and Bruce Cabot were facing her, and Arlene was a little off to her side—shouted out, "He's been playing that game longer than anyone here but me!" And then two great but somehow delicate hands rose behind Phil's and Frank's shoulders.

It was John Wayne.

Although Lillian had met him before, she wasn't prepared for the way he appeared to her this evening. All the people on his lawn, all the conversations begun in his name, all the attention to his person, reinforced his fame in a way that made her uncomfortable. She realized she had become the focal point of the little group because John Wayne stepped between Frank and Bruce Cabot in order to kiss her on the cheek. From there, he was introduced to Arlene and Phil.

Frank always straightened a little in Wayne's presence. His restless eyes became attentive, his sometimes vague body took shape, his big but anxious hands awaited instructions at his sides. It would be easy to demean him at a time like this, but Lillian never felt the urge. Wayne appealed to something in Frank that was more mysterious than his desire to please, more meaningful than his ambition to be a great man. She had to admit that being Duke's employee ennobled him, somehow.

John Wayne was always bigger than she had imagined. And so much more boyish. Her own husband had a bit of that kind of charm. But what Frank had a bit of, Duke had abundantly. In spite of his size, he was never sexually threatening. She couldn't imagine him having the kind of edge Bruce Cabot had. And therefore, at least for Lillian, he was attractive beyond all accounting.

"I guess I can always trust Bruce to find the prettiest ladies in the crowd. That's why I've been following him around for such a long time."

He took Frank's hand for the second time, as though he had forgotten the first or needed to reinforce it. "I'm glad you're here, Frank," he said.

Wayne was gracious to point out different aspects of his property that Frank had improved. Cabot looked a little dull with the fact that he was no longer the center of attention, but Phil and

Arlene were enormously pleased to be the object of this explanation—even though they had heard it earlier from Frank. They looked down the length of John Wayne's arm toward whatever he pointed at as though he were describing some great prize he'd just given them. Lillian was relieved that this moment had come for them—meeting John Wayne—and that they seemed to be enjoying themselves.

After Wayne left them—as everyone knew he would have to—Bruce Cabot wandered off as well. He did his best to reclaim the attention he had lost when Duke showed up, but it wasn't possible. Arlene glowed, and Lillian wasn't certain her friend understood that Duke was no longer with them. Phil watched Frank nervously. Lillian imagined that Phil was calculating what effect long exposure to Duke Wayne might have had on Frank's personality. For a moment, Phil seemed uncomfortable with envy. Lillian was just glad she didn't have to endure Bruce Cabot anymore, and she was looking forward to the rest of the party, as though Wayne's attention had relieved her of the desire to seek Wayne's attention. She was free to be enthusiastic about drinking and eating fancy food and recognizing movie stars.

She asked Frank to dance. Or rather, she *asked Frank to ask her* to dance. "Why don't you ask me to dance?" Frank was shocked, not by the circumlocution or his wife's presumption, but by the entire notion of dancing. He lifted his eyebrows as if to say, *Oh, we could do that, too, couldn't we?* Frank was a fine dancer who loved to show off at parties like this. A few moments earlier—although he hadn't noticed it—the twelve-piece orchestra on the patio beyond the pool had left off their moody the-party-is-just-starting music and moved into a swinging tune that Lillian liked but didn't recognize. If they hurried, they might be the first couple on the floor.

Fortunately for both of them, Frank was in his initial moments of boozy exuberance. Duke's appearance at his side had given him a push that scotch and soda would smooth into a glide which might last for the next few hours. Lillian recognized the "dramatic arc"—a term she had learned in her college lit class just a few weeks earlier—of her husband's drinking. At the moment, he was rising toward his zenith, and with any luck he might still be rising until it was time for him to go home.

As other couples began to gather around them, Lillian said, "It was nice of him to make Arlene and Phil feel at home. Sometimes he seems to me like such a good man."

"When did you ever think he wasn't a good man?" Frank asked.

"I guess I don't always like his movies."

Frank lifted his head to make certain no one was listening. "It's a funny time to talk about this," he said.

"No one will throw us out."

"No one but me." Frank smiled.

"I liked *True Grit*," Lillian conceded, "but you can have the rest of them. He always plays the same character—himself."

"You say that as if it were a bad thing. It's not a bad thing."

Lillian pulled Frank a little closer, set her cheek to his cheek, and whispered, "Okay, sweetheart."

After swinging through the rest of the tune that Lillian didn't recognize, the orchestra segued into "Do You Know the Way to San Jose?" which energized Frank into a glide and twist that made Lillian forget how much she despised the song. Frank caught her laughing as she imagined Arlene looking around the party for Burt Bacharach. The dance floor became thick with couples who must have loved the song, and Frank was forced to restrain himself a little, dance closer, concentrate harder. With Frank so firmly in control of her body, Lillian allowed her attention to wander through the other couples who shared the dance with them. Although it was still early in the party, one middle-aged man was acting out the song between disordered two-steps with his wife. When they got to the part where the singer sang,

"and all the stars
that never were
are parking cars
and pumping gas,"

he shuffled away from his wife and made a gesture with his hands as though he were paying someone from a stack of bills. The rest of the crowd was undistinguished. If a lot of stars had arrived at the party, none of them were dancing yet. But at the far end of the dancing area, near the swimming pool, a couple joined the music with such gentle confidence in their possession of the moment that Lillian imagined they might be celebrities whom she didn't recognize. Like many of the men at the party, this one had the kind of longish hair that looked a little dangerous touching the collar of his shirt. He was dark-featured and deeply tanned, and he had the kind of strong face that Lillian remembered from her youth. He was a city boy done well in California, she was sure of it. He was about Lillian's age, and he had the look of belonging to the movie industry even if he wasn't necessarily a star himself. The woman he led to the dance floor seemed a little older, but just as attractive. She was the kind of pleasantly buffered Nordic blonde whose hair and face seemed to have been designed for sunshine. She couldn't have been any more different from him. He was dark, maybe Mediterranean, and his gaze over his strong nose was terrifically focused.

Lillian thought, Maybe he's Jewish.

30

Whether he was Jewish or not, Lillian couldn't take her eyes off him, couldn't keep herself from wondering whether he was the husband of this woman or just her escort. Whether he was an actor or a writer. A lawyer or a businessman. As Frank turned her away from the couple, she followed them as best she could. He danced well, although not as well as Frank. Moment to moment, he seemed fearful that he might carry his partner away into a turn she wasn't prepared for. This made Lillian think again that she might not be his wife. He was reticent and unfamiliar like a bachelor. Maybe he was a homosexual. She didn't think she had ever met a homosexual in California, but she imagined that a Hollywood party—even one being held in Newport Beach—was likely to be full of them. He was concerned about himself—she could see by the way he wore his hair. Maybe he *is* queer. But then the strangest thought she'd had that evening entered her head. Lillian was often proud of her strange thoughts—they kept her separate from her husband and children, kept her sane deep within herself—but this one made her uneasy. Wouldn't he be what one of her Jewish boys would look like today? Couldn't she give one of them fourteen years and make him into such a man? Before she had a chance to completely scare the hell out of herself, the band moved into another tune and Frank pulled her in the opposite direction.

Although Frank was a wonderful dancer, he didn't have much endurance. He became bored and tired after a few songs. The crowd was getting a bit much for Lillian, too. She lost track of her urban-boy-done-well-in-California, and as a consequence, she lost interest in the dancing.

Frank wanted another drink, and they picked their way toward one of the five bars that studded the lawn. All around Lillian, the party was approaching its peak, and the noise insulating all of them from the night was layered like blankets on a bed. While

Frank drew her up to the bar, she tried to imagine herself sensitive enough to pull her friends out from that huge noise.

Lillian had already spent too much of her life watching men drink. And now it seemed to her that there had been years of her marriage devoted to nothing else. Giving Frank booze was a chemistry experiment: he could have a good night and be charming, he could have a bad night and become a thug. Different amounts had different effects on different nights.

And yet Lillian knew she had to let him go sometimes. And she had known even before they arrived at the party that this was going to be one of those nights. Children get to be greedy on Christmas morning. Grandparents get to be cranky on their vacations. Frank gets to be drunk during John Wayne's Christmas party. As much as she hated his drinking, she hoped that for tonight she could become that different kind of wife, the one who could tolerate, maybe even enjoy, his drinking.

Frank ordered a scotch and soda for himself and a Tom Collins for Lillian. It was maybe his fourth drink of the evening. As the bartender went to work, Frank addressed Lillian theatrically. "Duke has told each one of these guys that if they don't keep the drinkers happy, they will be shot at dawn." The bartender, perhaps true to his instructions from Duke, smiled warmly and accepted Frank's handshake.

Lillian took a sip of her Tom Collins, and it reminded her of how much she could enjoy booze if she ever allowed herself.

At that moment, as if he'd been cued, Duke Wayne himself appeared beside them at the bar; he had his big, rangy arm around the shoulder of Lillian's young man from the dance floor. Wayne smiled at Lillian in a way she believed was genuine. Lillian flattered herself that she could tell when a man liked her, and Wayne seemed to like her. She had seen the pleasure in his eyes, as though meeting her again meant more to him than he could easily say. Wayne pushed the young man in the direction of Frank. And then he took Lillian's hand.

"You throw a rock at this party and you're going to hit a couple of New Yorkers. But you three are the only ones that I really trust. Michael Grau, this is Frank and Lillian Barden. They're from the Bronx, you're from the Bronx. Michael's a big bean counter for Warner Brothers. Frank here built my whole fucking house again last year." Wayne's eyes widened and he looked a little startled. He hadn't yet let go of Lillian's hand, but now he took it up again in earnest. "I'm sorry, sweetheart, my foul mouth." Lillian nodded as though to excuse him, but he didn't let go of her hand.

"You two don't know each other already, do you?"

Michael put his hand on Duke's shoulder in a gesture Lillian would have thought presumptuous for a "bean counter" had not Michael done it with such tenderness. He said, "Duke, the Bronx is a very big place."

"Yeah, right." Duke let go of Lillian's hand. "But California's an even bigger place and I know half the people in the goddamn state."

He turned to take Lillian's hand again. She nodded in a gesture of forgiveness—she was starting to get the hang of this—which Duke must have understood because he aborted his apology, returned his attention to the men, and shook hands all around before leaving to rejoin the party.

Michael was a tall man, although not as tall as Frank. His tuxedo hung from his body as though it had been made for him, and it occurred to Lillian that maybe it *had* been. His body was still lean enough that she could imagine him as a twenty-three-year-old "bean counter" looking for a job in New York City. Her husband's body, poised between the two of them, bore much less relation to the body he'd had at twenty-three. He used to be sinewy, now he was just strong. Michael was more like Lillian herself: a tall drink of water.

Duke had left them with a man Lillian was afraid would patronize her husband. Maybe because she could imagine him as one of her suitors, she was worried that the movie business would look down on the construction business, that the obviously college-educated Michael would have fun with her thick-handed Frank. She was rallying herself to prevent that when she realized that Michael had *wanted* to meet them.

"You're an accountant?" Frank said, mindful of John Wayne's absence. "Maybe you're a CPA?"

"I haven't found the time to get my certification yet, but that's on the list. They keep pushing me up the ladder just the way I am, and sometimes I think I may never get my CPA. Sometimes I'm not sure I need it. You're a builder?"

"Framing. Room additions. Remodeling jobs like this one. Apartment buildings."

Lillian could already see the beginning of a problem as her husband tried to make himself comfortable. The apartment buildings part was not quite true. Wayne was talking to Frank about that, but it wasn't reality yet. Frank didn't yet know whether Michael was above him or below him in the hierarchy of the party. Frank had great difficulty with men who had been to college, and Michael had the kind of self-confidence that was often the result of a good degree.

Doing his best to figure out where he stood, Frank said, "It's exciting for Lillian and I to see all these movie stars in one place. Working in the picture business, you must be used to that by now."

Michael smiled. "Not too many people are interested in my income projections for their next film, but when they are, I guess I'm just as excited to shake hands with a movie star as the next fellow. I know Duke because he likes to stop by and poke his nose around the office when he's got a few days between pictures. Nobody really loves an accountant, but Duke seems to understand what we do better than most of them I've met."

"Who else do you know?" Lillian asked. She wished she hadn't. It wasn't a party question. It showed too much desire for an answer.

Michael just smiled, which made Lillian feel her embarrassment even more acutely. He shuffled his shoes along the pink concrete as though it wasn't necessary to display his connection to a world that Lillian would never be connected to. He stared down at his shiny black shoes and then, his smile a little darker, looked into Lillian's eyes. He patronized her so effortlessly it made her think that this was the real advantage of a college degree, that this was what Frank had always envied about men like Michael.

Frank, lost from the conversation for almost a minute, taking stock of the swelling crowd, taking stock—again—of his improvements to the Wayne hacienda, said, "One really good way to get to know a man is to remodel his house."

"I imagine that's probably a very good way," Michael said.

And then Frank left them because he had to: Lillian recognized the landscape of her husband's drinking. He was entering a long plateau characterized by restlessness and bold sentences that defied the context of conversation. It was the time when he often left her alone at parties.

"I'm going to go find Phil and Arlene," Frank said.

Michael was surprised to be so suddenly alone with Lillian. She wouldn't have expected that. He searched his jacket for pockets which were sewn shut; and then, having met that obstacle, decided to invest his hands in the pockets of his pants, ruining the line of his beautifully tailored jacket.

"I liked this house the first time I saw it," Michael said. "I remember asking myself what a fellow like Duke would have to do to keep a house looking so good. And now I know: he gets someone smart like Frank to rebuild it every few years."

Lillian didn't like the sound of that, and she was determined to change the subject. "What part of the Bronx did you grow up in?"

"Parkchester mostly. My parents moved us to Manhattan for a while when Dad was doing well, but we always seemed to return to Parkchester. You?"

"My family never left the Bronx," Lillian said. "We made one apartment change from one block to another, and that was it. I never even had my own bedroom until I moved in with my husband."

"What part of the Bronx?"

"Around Castle Hill. East 177th Street."

"You wouldn't call that Parkchester?"

"I guess you could call it Parkchester. I never thought about it as Parkchester. Parkchester seems so . . . you know what I mean."

"I *think* I know what you mean."

"High school," Lillian said. "What high school did you go to?"

"Bronx High School of Science."

"I'm impressed."

"You should be. I worked my ass off. And you?"

"You won't be impressed."

"Try me."

36

"James Monroe."

"You're right. I'm not impressed."

"I was valedictorian, though."

"Okay, I'm impressed."

"I'm glad I've impressed you with something."

"Oh, you've been impressing me with many things. You've been impressing me since I first saw you on the dance floor."

"Are you flirting with me?"

"Of course I'm flirting with you," Michael said. "That's why they invite me to these parties, to flirt with people like you. You don't think they invited me because I'm a powerhouse in the movie industry?"

Lillian smiled. "I don't know why, but it's a real pleasure to speak with you."

"You know why."

"Okay. I get the feeling that you don't care what I think of you. Somehow, that's pleasant."

"On the contrary," Michael said. "It's myself that I'm insensitive to. You I care about a lot."

Talking this way, more than anything else about the party, was making Lillian happy. Among this sea of smiling faces and sweetly expensive finger food and bright drinks, she had almost forgotten how sharp a conversation could be.

Michael turned from her toward the crowd beyond the bar. He surveyed it as though it were a house he was afraid to enter. By now, famous people were standing everywhere, providing the significance that the party needed to be considered successful by people like Arlene and Frank and Phil. Lillian stood apart from all that now. Her conversation with Michael had set her in a different place entirely. Now that it was completely night, the red-and-white-striped tent seemed to be stealing color from the guests beneath it. Lillian imagined she could see the compliments and the flirtations and the back talk, all of it accumulating beneath that circus tent, mixing all around with the cigarette smoke and the smell of good booze. Michael stood, just looking into the crowd, for much longer than Lillian felt comfortable. Either he would talk to her soon or she would have to leave and look for her friends.

"I dated guys like you before I married Frank," Lillian said.

That did it. He turned around. "And what do you mean by *guys like me?*"

"Smart alecks, fellows who couldn't contain their energy in the normal ways, so that it was always leaking out in ways that made other people uncomfortable. Frank beat up a guy like you once. He was just smarting off and trying to make Frank feel stupid. The guy was hitting on me, too, but I never told Frank that. Frank was drunk and he might have killed him."

"Why do I get the feeling that we're talking about something else here? What are we talking about?"

"We're talking about the fact that I've always liked smart alecks but I didn't marry one. I married a guy who beats up smart alecks."

"You don't think I can take care of myself? Do I look *feeble* to you?"

"You look fine," Lillian said. "I'm just talking, trying to draw you back into the conversation."

"You're doing a good job."

"I was afraid you were about to leave," she said. "I'm not ready to talk with anyone else."

"I'm here," Michael said. "You know, I've met guys like your husband before, too. I *like* guys like your husband. Some of my best friends were Irish Catholic thugs. I like to think of myself as a Jewish thug."

38

"You don't look like a thug."

"Do I look Jewish?"

"Yes, you do."

"Frank doesn't look like a thug, either," Michael said.

"No, he doesn't."

"Let's see. I imagine he's the kind of man who hates blacks and is wary of Jews on principle, but he makes lots of exceptions for the people he meets. All blacks are lazy except for *my* friends. All Jews are greedy except for *my* friends. Am I in the ballpark?"

"Yes, you are." Although she had certainly courted it, Lillian wasn't prepared for this kind of honesty.

"How about you?" Michael asked. "How do you feel about Jews, Miss Lillian?"

"I like them fine. I grew up in the Bronx, didn't I?"

"That doesn't mean anything. And if you'd really grown up in the Bronx, you'd know that doesn't mean anything."

"You're right. I'm sorry."

"So how was it? Would your mother let you date a Jewish boy?"

"Of course she would."

"Marry one?"

"Nope."

"What if she thought you were . . . you know, behind her back?"

"It never came anywhere near that."

Michael smiled. He must have felt as though she'd made an enormous concession. Lillian knew that it wasn't much of a concession at all.

"So then I could have been the boy that you *didn't* marry. I could have even been the boy that you didn't sleep with. I could be the bitter bachelor who you passed up because of the prejudices of your parents. Couldn't I?"

"Parent. Only one."

"Couldn't I?"

"Yes, maybe you could. But you're not."

"Don't be so sure, Lillian."

At that moment, Arlene emerged from the crowd. Somehow, both her complexion and her cocktail dress were more vibrant than they had been earlier that evening. She'd been drinking, that was for sure. But then again, so had Lillian. She'd found that if she set down her Tom Collins and smiled at the bartender, she didn't even have to ask for another.

"Arlene, this is Michael. He grew up in the same neighborhood as Frank and I. We were just talking about how much we both like California."

Arlene lifted her eyebrows. *Oh really?* She was reaching for an affect that was almost beyond her.

"But we didn't know each other when we still lived in the Bronx. We just met here a few minutes ago. Duke introduced us. Where's Frank anyway?"

Michael shook Arlene's hand and told her he was pleased to meet her.

"Frank's over by the bay designing houses for anyone who wants one."

"Phil?"

"Phil's helping Frank design the houses. And what do you do?" Arlene asked Michael.

"I'm an accountant," Michael replied.

"Are you Mr. Wayne's accountant?"

"Not exactly." Michael smiled coolly. "I keep an eye on

things for Warner Brothers, where Mr. Wayne has made a few of his pictures."

"Warner Brothers?"

"Yes."

"That must be really interesting."

"You really think so?"

"Arlene really thinks so," Lillian offered. "She's probably more fascinated by you than anyone she's met at the party."

"Yeah," Arlene said. "I think I can see by the cut of your jacket that you're an accountant's accountant, right? You're one of the *big* accountants."

"Either that or I rented a very expensive tuxedo." Michael smiled. "Yes, I guess you could say that. I've worked hard."

"Well, tell me," Arlene said. "Do folks court you? I mean, I'm guessing that a smart person would court you. You have the power of the pen. Looking at the numbers one way or another, you could probably make or break someone's career."

"Numbers don't lie, Arlene."

Arlene made a face that said loudly and clearly, *Don't treat me like a boob from Lompoc, California.*

Michael caught her look and relented. Actually, he seemed a little ashamed of himself for underestimating her. "The numbers can be squeezed a bit, I guess. I don't do it on purpose. Sometimes an executive will ask me to do it. Sometimes I'm just . . . well . . . *in favor* of someone's success and I notice somewhere down the line that I wasn't as objective as I might have been."

"That's more like it," Arlene said. "I guessed that."

Just then Frank returned with Phil in tow. They were both showing the effects of drink, but they managed to draw a circle around Lillian and Arlene that excluded Michael.

While Lillian's attention was with her husband—while she tried to gauge where he was in the evening's adventure—Michael drifted toward another group of people a few yards away. Hugs and kisses and handshakes welcomed his drift. She was surprised to discover that he had left so quickly, but she imagined it was for the best. She didn't want to spend her time at this fancy party comparing a man she hardly knew—Michael—to a man she knew too well—Frank. She hoped her life could be bigger than that.

Frank and Phil coaxed their wives away from the bar, and they all sat down in patio chairs beside a glass table. The commotion in Lillian's head didn't die down quickly. Her husband saw to that.

"And now where is your friend from the Bronx?" Frank asked.

"He's just over there," Lillian said.

"I'm guessing he left at just the moment we returned. Am I right?"

Lillian said nothing. Frank checked the distance between himself and Michael. "We probably shouldn't turn our back on him, Phil. He might try to poke us up the ass."

Among the men she had grown up with—and Frank was one of them—a certain level of drunkenness always brought on talk of homosexuality. It was as certain as wetness after rain.

"Frank," Lillian admonished.

"He's a homo," Frank said. "I don't blame him for it. God makes mistakes."

"Keep your voice down."

Drunkenness had increased Frank's catalogue of facial expressions as well. He dropped his chin and looked at his wife from under his wide and severe brow as if to say, *I'll pretend I didn't hear*

42

that. For a quick moment, booze had turned her husband into an expressive individual.

Lillian began to speak to Arlene, and by the time she finished, Frank and Phil were off again, looking for someone to talk to who wouldn't confuse them by talking back.

She heard his voice before she saw his face. His voice had already become familiar to her. She thought she could imagine how California had softened it, although she knew that it was probably as hard as it had ever been in the Bronx.

"So what would we have been like, dating each other in our green youth?"

Lillian turned and so did Arlene. He had come up behind them, seated himself in a chair, and now looked as though he had all the time in the world. Arlene was more amused than Lillian, and perhaps as a concession to the way good booze made her feel—less like a housewife from Lompoc and more like a beatnik schoolgirl—she turned to Michael and told him what it would have been like.

"Lillian would have worried that you were a little too fast and experienced for her. She would have kept you within strict boundaries for the longest time. You would have been lucky to get your tongue in her mouth by the seventh date."

"Jesus, Arlene!" Lillian said.

"It's the truth, honey."

"But after she'd learned to trust me," Michael said. "How would we have been then?"

"You would have told her—because this was the kind of kid *you* were—that so long as you were dating her, you would never take her to the same restaurant twice. In fact, you would tell her, I'll never even take you to a *similar* restaurant twice. Always a new and interesting restaurant for you two. It would have been one of the main things that convinced her to keep going out with you."

Lillian remembered this. It was, in fact, how Frank had courted her, and it was for a while the only reason why she continued to see him—her wonder at the way he could keep producing these small romantic restaurants with great food. She was certain she had never told Arlene about any of this.

"How did I keep it up? All those restaurants?" Michael asked.

"How the hell should I know?" Arlene laughed. "It's not my fucking story."

"I kept it up," Michael answered his own question, "because I had lots of friends and business acquaintances already, and at the end of *any* conversation with *anyone,* I would ask them about their favorite places to eat in the city."

Lillian was surprised again. It was becoming too convincing.

"And what happened as things moved along?" Arlene asked. "Did your friendship . . . *deepen?*"

"I was conscious of the fact that I was dating someone who had to be taken seriously," he said. "Let's just say that I was an attractive young man with some money in my pocket . . ."

"Let's just say that," Lillian added sarcastically.

". . . and I'd been dating more than a few women for longer than a while, but after I met Lillian, I had this big sense within myself that I was entering a project which wouldn't yield to fifty percent of my effort, wouldn't even, for that matter, yield to ninety-seven percent of my effort. I had to give her all of my attention or I wasn't going to get anywhere with this thing."

"This thing?" Lillian said. *"This thing?* You're talking about human beings, not a cost-benefit analysis."

"What are you so angry about?" Michael smiled.

"I don't like the way you're talking about me."

"Are we talking about you?"

"Hypothetically, you're talking about me," Lillian said. "I mean, you're imagining something about me, and I don't like the way you're doing it."

"Tell me where I'm wrong. How should we be telling this story differently?"

"Well, it's not as though I was some block of marble that you had to carve a woman out of. Maybe I wanted to be courted as much as you wanted to court me. Maybe I had some thoughts about you long before you started all the fancy maneuvers."

"And what did you think?" Michael said. "What did you decide about me?"

"I don't know what I thought!" Lillian said. "This isn't about a real person. This isn't about me. I'm just saying that you should think harder about what the woman wanted, about her point of view."

"For years, that was *all* I thought about," Michael said.

Arlene, who suddenly seemed impatient with a conversation that threatened to leave her out, directed the question back to Michael, who seemed a little confused in the aftermath of arguing with Lillian.

"What did *you* want?" Arlene asked him. "What was *your* objective?"

"I wanted everything," Michael announced. "My objective was Lillian Rose Hedendal herself, that sweet Swedish smarty-pants from the wrong side of the tracks, that tall drink of water, her skinny legs poured into slacks, her face always on the edge of a heartbreaking frown. I wanted Lillian."

45

God help me, Lillian thought. Jesus Christ, help me. It wasn't quite a prayer, but it was as close as she'd come in years.

The party, having grown and prospered for several hours, was now beginning to recede. The three of them had become quiet, too. For the first time in the last half hour, Lillian could see her husband. Frank was across the lawn talking to a man who looked like Dean Martin but probably wasn't Dean Martin. Something she'd heard in school the week before came back to her with the force of revelation—something Professor Wolman had said as an aside before he began in earnest his stultifying examination of the role of hats in Conrad's novels. "Bing Crosby has always seemed like an evil man, don't you think?"

She knew that her mind was only capable of such tricks, such wildness, because she was near Michael. He was watching her at just that moment. Maybe they *had* loved each other at some time in the past, way back in a life she was no longer connected to. Why couldn't she remember? She guessed that anything was possible. She remembered that time she'd gone to a consciousness-raising group for women who were married to alcoholics. Alanon. She'd gone only once, but she'd heard a woman describe her inability to *accept* the extent of her husband's drinking, her incredible *denial* of the fact that it was ruining her family life. Lillian felt close to that woman. Maybe, Lillian thought, I have lost a part of my life because I am too afraid to look at it?

And then Michael asked her to dance.

She could imagine being shocked by his request because it crossed a line she hadn't intended to cross. She could imagine being delighted by his request because it was just the kind of intimacy she had been hoping for. As it was, she was neither shocked nor delighted. It was, rather, as if the whole thing had already happened and she were just putting her body in a place where it had already been.

Now that the party was waning, only three or four couples pushed each other around the dance floor beside the pool. Michael was a tall man, but no taller than Lillian. It seemed like a luxury to look into his eyes, to be looking neither up nor down at a man. Michael was not a dancer the way her husband Frank was a dancer. Even when Michael took her along the rough edges of a song the way Frank did, it was with a sense that he would give her only as much as she wanted. Lillian didn't know how much she wanted. She became afraid the other dancers would recognize her small contentment to be in Michael's arms for what it was.

"It takes you a little while to relax, doesn't it?" Michael asked.

"I'm still not relaxed. I feel like I'm dancing with an old boyfriend and my husband's watching me with daggers in his eyes."

"Daggers in his eyes?" Michael laughed.

"Yes."

"Is your husband watching you?"

"No, I don't know where he is. I saw him a few minutes ago, but now he's off somewhere."

"It seems like he's been off somewhere all evening."

"Yes."

"And you feel like you're dancing with an old boyfriend?"

"I *am* dancing with an old boyfriend. That's what you told me, isn't it?"

"That's right."

The band went from "Fly Me to the Moon" into "Yesterday." The Beatles were about as racy as they got all evening.

Maybe now that things were starting to wind down and people were thinking about going home, the bandleader felt he could risk a tune that didn't concede so much to the taste of the host, who had a hard time thinking about music unless it was made by a man or woman whose hand he'd shaken.

Lillian loved that song. She sang it to herself around her kitchen. She'd heard her children singing it. Once, when she was on her way to the allergist's office with her oldest son—he had such bad asthma, he was allergic to so many things—she pulled her red Dodge Dart to the side of the road so that she could listen without losing part of the song to her nervous concentration on the road. As she sang along, her son watched as though he didn't recognize her. And, really, she didn't recognize herself. Seeing that uncomplicated joy reflected in her son's distrusting eyes, she wanted to leave the car and walk away from her life forever. She felt like that now with Michael, as though two more moments of happiness might kill her.

When one of the four other couples left the dance floor, Lillian found her excuse. She begged off the rest of the dance with some words about leaving Arlene alone that she didn't even hear herself speak. She hated this part of herself—the schmaltzy, heart-broken-to-pieces-like-a-little-girl part. She didn't know who she might become in Michael's arms, but she wasn't ready to find out.

When they returned to the table, Arlene still seemed happy and drunk. She was watching the party as though it were her television set. She had her cigarettes out and she had another drink and she didn't care who knew about it. When someone who looked rich or famous passed her table, her eyes followed them frankly, as though they were plates of food she might order if only she knew the names.

Lillian sat down, but Michael didn't. He stood in front of

Arlene, his feet spread like an American man's, his hands in his pockets.

"And then what happened?" Michael asked. The glibness was gone. He really wanted to know.

"What are we talking about?" Arlene asked.

"What happened between Lillian and Michael."

"What happened was . . ." Arlene engaged him as well as she could, despite her suddenly increasing drunkenness. "What happened then was she met Frank, and she realized that she couldn't go out with anyone anymore that she liked as much as she liked you."

When they located Frank and Phil among the ruins of the party, the two men were sitting on a couch together in John Wayne's living room watching a group of certainly more famous and powerful men play poker at a table near the center of the room. Phil was falling asleep, but Frank watched the progress of the game as though his livelihood depended on it, which it did not because he wasn't playing the game. Arlene cleared up that point right off. "Why aren't *you* playing?" she asked her husband and her good friend Frank.

"We don't know how to play," Phil admitted.

Oblivious to both Arlene's question and Phil's answer, Frank continued to watch the game.

Lillian, coming from behind Arlene through the sliding glass door that opened the living room to Newport Bay, saw three men she recognized and five she didn't. Duke Wayne was there, as were Bruce Cabot and Johnny Weissmuller. Another five men played, but their features—because their faces were not known to Lillian—washed together like so many patrons of a Wild West saloon, sitting in the midst of action but somehow never part of the action. John Wayne looked more like an ordinary mortal man than she had ever seen him. Like all the rest of the men at the card table—actually four card tables pushed together—he smoked a cigarette. His toupee had abandoned his head, and thatches of unkempt hair from the sides crawled over his clean dome as though they were trying to recapture lost territory. His hands, holding his cards before the reading glasses on the end of his great nose, were liver-spotted and looked as though they had been tanned by fire rather than sun. When Lillian and Arlene came through the door, he recognized them over the frames of his glasses. He smiled at them. He winked.

Her own husband hadn't noticed her entering the room, but John Wayne did. She remembered something she'd read in a romance novel late at night, after Frank's tortured snoring and terrifying mumbles of fear had woken her up: "Each sadness reminded her of all the other sadnesses that had preceded it." Lillian didn't want to be in this room right now, and even John Wayne's wink wasn't much consolation.

She sat beside her husband on the couch. She put her hand over his big hand, great like John Wayne's hands were great, but not as old and maybe a little damaged by carpentry, not as perfect as an actor's hands could be.

"Frank, we're all tired. Don't you think it's time we went home?"

At first, he didn't acknowledge her. He continued to watch sharp cards slice the air between big men. Weissmuller, whom Lillian had enjoyed when she was a girl, said, "There will be a hell of a price to pay for that. Let's thank God most of us can afford it." John Wayne watched his cards and then watched Weissmuller before saying, "Maybe *you* can afford it, boss, but I still need to work for a living."

"Come on, Frank," she whispered. "Can we go home now?"

Frank continued to ignore her. Lillian thought, We are trained from birth to find them beautiful, but they are not beautiful. Children are beautiful. Often, young women are beautiful as wild horses and well-bred dogs and considerate zoo creatures are beautiful. But men are not beautiful. They are boxes that fill up with toil and regret and anger. And if women were that way, too—and Lillian guessed that they were—at least women got to keep the dignity that came along with loving their children more than themselves. Most men never experienced that much dignity in their whole lives.

"Pay attention to me," she said.

Frank turned to her, and uncertainly lifting his hand to her knee, he shook it violently for a second and said, "We're going to stay here and watch these boys play poker for a while." His eyes were blue. His gaze held Lillian precisely. And he was as dead drunk as she'd ever seen him while he was still able to speak.

"What do you mean *we?*" she said. *"We're* getting tired, *we* want to go home." It occurred to her that he was a sick man. His dead eyes had told her that, but she couldn't keep the thought. She had imagined for a moment that this might not be the best tone to approach him with, but she couldn't keep that thought, either. She guessed that she should be embarrassed to fight with her husband in front of John Wayne, but she wasn't.

He shook her knee again, this time returning his eyes to the card game across the room, this time more gently, although his hands seemed palsied to her; his hands vibrated like an old drunk's. "You calm down, honey," he spoke quietly. "You calm the fuck down."

She stood up from the couch, but almost before she could,

51

Frank's hand had reached after her to restrain her. He held her wrist without pulling her back down, as though he hoped the energy of her anger would lift him with her. Phil and Arlene looked away. No one else seemed to notice.

"She wants to get back out and see her Jew boy." Frank spoke to Arlene, although Arlene was studiously ignoring him, watching the drapes, watching the harbor lights just beyond the living room drapes. "I know things about her that the Jew boy will never know. I know that she's no good in bed. I know she wishes . . . I know that she's a fucking . . ."

His brain seized up for a moment, choking on all the alcohol and resentment. He coughed like a diver too grateful for air. He spit out half-formed words like teeth before he coughed once hard, and then asked Phil, with half his breath, "You could see that guy was queer, couldn't you? You could see that guy was a fucking fruit?"

Phil looked terrified, but he nodded. It was the most conviction he could risk under these circumstances. Lillian snapped her hand out of Frank's grasp. Frank didn't react. He seemed pleased to have his own hand back.

"Just let me have the fucking car, Frank. Give me the ticket. You can find some way to get home."

She held out her hand as though the gesture had some kind of weight for him, as though he were her smallest child and might be cajoled into cooperation.

The poker players acted as though they were used to such displays. Indeed, they probably were. The scene gathered familiarity for Lillian as she realized that this was often the way it was in a Wild West saloon. No matter what mayhem might be worked out near the center of the room, the chances were good that a poker game might continue somewhere in a corner. The men around

52

John Wayne flipped cards and shuffled and moved chips, but they didn't speak quite as loudly once the Bardens began to fight. Bruce Cabot, supremely unperturbed by the scene, even ordered himself another screwdriver at precisely the moment when Lillian seemed in the most danger of being struck by her husband. John Wayne, exercising his prerogative as host of the party and master of the house, cast his eyes in Frank's direction from moment to moment as though he were encouraging him *not* to strike his wife. Maybe Wayne knew what most heavy drinkers knew: it wasn't the man who made a lot of noise who became violent, but the man who didn't make much noise at all.

Frank wasn't making much noise.

"Why don't you *walk* home, you skinny slut?" he whispered.

Lillian felt as though her soul had been smuggled out of the world. A peculiar calm settled over every object in the room, as though the earth had lost its soul as well. Ashtrays and highball glasses, cigarette cases and novelty cuff links, a small sculpture by Remington in the corner and the way Arlene's dress fluttered over her skin as an unexpected breeze blew in from the bay—all of it seemed to Lillian like the day after a bombing in which many small children had died. She looked around at the men who played poker—"supernumeraries," her professor would have called them, "spearcarriers" in spite of fame or power—and she saw in each of their faces the same qualities: an empty discipline and an astounding lack of warmth.

John Wayne straightened in his chair. He had short legs for a man his size, and therefore he was a taller man sitting down than he was standing up. He had been sitting low in his chair so that he wouldn't have to look down so much on the other card players. Lillian was no longer watching for the light behind his eyes when he said, "Lillian, let Frank stay and play poker with us for a while.

He can drive home in my car, and that way you folks can leave just as soon as you want."

She couldn't bear to look at John Wayne. She continued to face her husband. She said, "Give me the ticket, Frank."

And his soul did not return to his eyes as he offered up his independence from the pocket of his rented blue tuxedo.

As Lillian drove above the ditch that would one day become the newest segment of the San Diego Freeway, she wondered aloud at the word she had first heard when she was twelve years old.

"Anarchy."

They were all three of them too tired. Phil and Arlene hadn't responded to the word, and this made Lillian question whether she'd even said it. She was thinking about that time in the attorney's office as she sat waiting to meet her father, her two sisters beside her, stiff as dolls. The humidity of a late summer day in New York City prickled their backsides on the leather couch, but not one of them wanted to admit that she was uncomfortable. The smartly dressed lawyer who had taken their deposition—and would now take them to see the judge—had left his office door open. Lillian watched him skip across the room to give his secretary a piece of paper, and he said, "There could end up being *anarchy* if we don't get this out of the office by tonight." Then, as now, Lillian let the word stand between the back of her throat and the tip of her tongue. There was magic in a word that she didn't yet know the meaning of. She scooted a little across the leather and tipped her head to see inside the lawyer's door before it closed, but she learned nothing else.

Now, leaving behind the hardscrabble construction of New-port Boulevard for the cosmic ease and unthinking gravity of the newly built Newport Freeway, her mind was painting itself with all the troubling colors that the word brought to her. Her father's face in the judge's chambers was the color of her palm after she'd been making a fist. Her father's hair was blond like dead grass. Her mother's eyes looking at him were brown and astonishing like shit discovered under your heel. As they passed through Irvine, Phil pointed at the ancient blimp hangars that dominated the Marine Corps Air Station and said the same thing he must have said on the way out to John Wayne's party.

"Huge!"

The judge had wanted to know what the children thought of their father, what it was like to live with just their mother, if there was anything the judge could do to improve the quality of their lives. He was an odd but not so very old man, maybe even near her father's age. He obviously enjoyed talking to children, although he wasn't good at it. He asked long, complicated questions when simple ones would have been better. He even asked simple questions that the children couldn't understand. He tried to reassure each of the little girls by touching them, but neither Lillian nor her sisters enjoyed being touched. Lillian's mother later called him "that relentless little faggot" in a burst of profanity unnatural to her tight little mouth. Although the judge was willing to recognize the evil that had been done by Lillian's father, he didn't extend himself too much in making good of it. At one point, he asked all three children, "Don't you think you would be happier if you could spend some more time with your daddy?" Lillian could feel the air around her mother stiffen, and Lillian was afraid that her own fine white teeth would come flying out of her mouth if she only opened her lips to speak.

Phil repeated himself. "Huge!"

Nothing ever turned out the way she imagined it. And Lillian had a good imagination. Neighborhoods that should have been green and full of lush, bursting trees became neighborhoods that were dry with concrete which was too clean and new, and the few trees there were had to be supported by stakes. Tonight, of all nights, she didn't want to become the kind of woman who regretted her life. But there it was: she regretted her life. The world, which had been so full of her ambition for herself and her family, now seemed empty and "incomplete," like the newly built homes that filled the field beside their house on Milford Road. She had wanted to become more than she was, and maybe that was the precise nature of her sin. Until tonight, she hadn't known herself well enough to understand that these notions were more smoke than fire, more dust than brick, more shudder than real movement in a real direction. If someone were to ask her, she wouldn't be able to tell him what she'd made with her life. The easy consolation of three children and a home seemed like shit to her. She wanted another context and there just wasn't any.

"Huge!"

Orange County was growing all around her, but except for those blimp hangars which Phil couldn't get unstuck from his drunken imagination, there was none of it taller than three stories. It wasn't like Manhattan, it wasn't even like the Bronx. Orange County was a short-pile carpet of concrete and wood that the giants of the earth had flopped over the dry desert of Southern California. Lillian had the sense that they could pull it back from the earth whenever they wanted. Although she remembered how much she had hated living there, how much she hated the bonds of family and an old world, New York City was durable in a way California would never be. Back East was where great hard fists of brick adhered to an earth that was solid like the screaming pain of labor, solid like the hardness of hope and the grinding of great dreams.

As they passed out of sight of the blimp hangars, she turned to see if Phil would say it again. He did not.

Arlene smiled, and then, as if called to defend Southern California by a force she was too human to understand, she roused from her highway hypnosis into a sense of herself as the person in the car who had been assigned to keep Lillian happy and alert.

"It sure was a nice party," Arlene said. "And I wasn't scared of anyone there. Do you think that was really Dean Martin? Or just someone who looked like him?"

The Long

Voyage Home

1939

When Marlene Dietrich first saw John Wayne, he was wearing a suit. This was at the Universal Pictures commissary in the late thirties, before John Wayne *was* John Wayne. Duke wore a suit because he wasn't in production. Dietrich, in a suit that cost a lot more than Wayne's, watched him from across the room. Her agent,

Charlie Feldman, sat beside her. As she finished chewing a spear of asparagus dipped in hollandaise sauce, she condescended to smile in a way that had already brought her to Hollywood, had already made her more money than the rest of the employees in the commissary put together. She watched John Wayne (he looked good in suits, but not so good in ties—he wore the suit without the tie, the collar buttoned to his neck) and she said, "Charlie, I've just seen what I want for Christmas."

Wayne was younger than Dietrich. Wayne was less successful. Wayne was married.

A few days after that, an actor named Rick Rorbach offered to lend Duke a bicycle to get around the studio. Duke was embarrassed because he couldn't remember Rick's screen name—he'd never seen any of his movies—and he wasn't too interested in bicycles. Duke Wayne wasn't one to keep up with the fads of the younger actors. He'd always been more comfortable with the older men around town. Except for his buddy from USC, Ward Bond, Duke's friends were the stuntmen, character actors, and directors. At that time, he was tight enough with John Ford that Ford took both him and Bond out for Catalina weekends aboard his sailboat, the *Araner*. Besides, Rorbach seemed fruity and Duke was afraid there was more to the offer than just a ride on a bike.

But Rorbach was persistent. Finally, as Duke was never in the mood to make an enemy, he accepted Rorbach's bike for an afternoon. It was great! He enjoyed rolling around the sets and warehouses so much that he was ashamed for judging Rorbach. Rick's a good guy, Duke thought as his muscles relaxed into the gentle repetition. He needed to stop worrying. His career would take off again soon.

She stepped out from behind a warehouse and stood in his path, not ignorant of the danger of his bearing down on her but choosing to disregard it. She stared straight into his eyes as the bike stuttered to a stop.

She said she wanted a ride. He said, "Miss Dietrich."

Duke was between the first two movies he would make for his friend John Ford—*Stagecoach* and *The Long Voyage Home*—and he was beginning to want success as he had never wanted it before. He was thirty-three years old, the age Christ was when he died, and sometimes Duke would walk around the studio making himself crazy by repeating, "I am now almost dead. I am now almost crucified. Herbert Yates has sent me to Calvary." Yates, his boss at Republic, refused to release him from the B Westerns that *Stagecoach* proved he had grown beyond. Duke had worked harder than any actor he knew, and he could feel his chance—the chance that John Ford had given him—slipping away as the months passed and the public memory of *Stagecoach* faded.

At first, he didn't think she was pretty. His friends would never believe this, but it was true. He'd seen her on the screen and around the lot, and her face had always seemed like a mask. In certain light and under certain circumstances, she looked like the stunned survivor of a catastrophe. Her cheekbones were too close to the surface of her skin. Her eyes were too intense. She wasn't the kind of woman he could imagine sleeping with. He liked his women softer.

And so it surprised Duke that he was being pulled in. After the first encounter on the bicycle, her face and body began to inhabit his imagination. One night after putting his children to bed—there were two of them then—he became so aroused by just

61

the thought of her that he drove to the market for a carton of cigarettes so he wouldn't have to be alone with his wife. After that difficult night, it seemed inevitable that he would see her again.

It started in an apartment her agent kept near the studio. Meeting in a restaurant would have made Duke more comfortable. Her agent's apartment was small but luxurious, and the interior design left Duke feeling that he was about to commit a bigger sin than he had planned on.

Marlene said, "Are you afraid of me? I can't believe you're afraid of me."

He could smile because he knew it wasn't true the way she imagined it. "I don't like this apartment." He set down his drink. "I want to be somewhere else."

"Where do you want to be, Mr. Duke Wayne?"

"Baja California. I want to be on a beach in Baja with the sun shining bright and the surf just big enough to hurt me."

"We can go there." Marlene smiled. "I think I would like to go there."

"Good. You can watch me bodysurf," Duke said. "You can watch me try to kill myself with the Pacific Ocean."

She arched her eyebrows and set down her drink. Duke guessed that she didn't know what he was talking about. "You make your body into a plane." He flattened his hand to demonstrate. "And you let the wave carry you into shore. I could show you how to do it, but you'd have to be a really good swimmer. Are you a really good swimmer?"

"I swim well," Marlene said. "In fact, I am a better swimmer than any man I've met, although I know nothing of bodysurfing. If you could teach me, that would be very nice. Maybe there will be something that I can teach you someday."

"Sure," Duke said. "Sure." At that moment, he touched her hand.

When he kissed her, a warm freedom spread from his chest into all his limbs. And when he lifted her from the couch, her weight in his arms was sweet, like carrying a baby. When he entered her body a few minutes later, he wanted to cry and tell her that everything he'd ever had was hers. Everything he'd ever hoped to have.

It wasn't just success Duke wanted; it was transcendence. He had thought John Ford could do that for him, could take him *beyond* himself. For a moment, as he watched *Stagecoach* in an audience of delighted fans, he could feel what that would be like. But the feeling went away just as quickly as it came.

To be forever outside of what he wanted with all his heart— Duke knew that this was an *American* feeling. Ford had taught him that; Ford knew that better than anyone. Wanting to be Indians, we had to kill them. Wanting the continent, we wrapped it into parcels and sold it away. And now, wanting to make movies about how pure we had been, we made movies that dripped with the sour residue of commerce. At the moments in his life when Duke should have felt triumph bouncing through his body like a drug, he felt empty and alone. Like an American, he wanted what he couldn't have.

Once, Marlene told him that America was a cow the Northern Europeans wanted to tip over. Another time, she told him the studio system was a too-ripe Southern California orange that intoxicated everyone who drank from it. More than once, she said that true sexual passion was as offensive to the world as an automobile driven by an infant. He didn't always understand her metaphors, but he only asked for explanation when he guessed it was too important not to ask.

They had been seeing each other for six months. They had left off meeting at Charlie Feldman's pied-à-terre, and Duke would rent a room in a discreet Beverly Hills hotel. Charlie Feldman was now his agent as well—thanks to Marlene—and Duke had a little more money in his pocket, thanks to a new contract that Charlie had negotiated. As Duke's career advanced, it became easier to explain long absences from his family. Marlene and Duke had taken weekend trips together, although not yet to Baja. They had even made a lousy film together called *Seven Sinners*. Now Duke paid for everything, and if Marlene spoke against this, even hinted at the inequity between their salaries, he would put a long, well-made finger to her lips and shush her as though she were his daughter objecting to an unfair bedtime.

She confessed to him one night that she felt like she'd skipped from the ruin of one empire to the ruin of another, that she was nothing but a camera whore in Germany or America. It was just after dusk and they talked in the hotel room without turning on the lights. Of course, Duke told her this wasn't true— that she was an artist, that she had great talent—but she just smiled at him with her mixture of amusement and contempt and motherly lust. She licked her fingers and smoothed his eyebrows into fine dark arches. She teased him that with such a lovely face, he could *still* be a singing cowboy.

Irritated and lustful, Duke wrestled her to the floor and kissed her pouty Northern European mouth. An erection pressed against his trousers, and he thought—for just a second—about how good it would feel to make war against an enemy as arrogant and powerful as Germany. Watching for signs in her boney face, his heart now full of tenderness, he said, "I would give you anything I have, I would *do* anything to keep feeling like this." The moment passed and another moment took its place. Marlene ran her fingers through his hair and kissed him hard before she let her head settle back into the carpet.

"Don't say that," she whispered.

"Why not?"

"Because it makes you sound like an asshole."

Ward Bond told Duke that Miss Dietrich was a lesbian—and Duke had heard that rumor—but Ward *liked* the idea and imagined that Duke would like it, too. Ward thought there was something special about sleeping with a lesbian—a conquest, an adventure that other men had been denied. Ward was also fond of the word "dyke," and enjoyed teasing his friend by saying, "Duke can't get his dick out of the dyke." It disgusted Duke to think about homosexuality— Marlene's or anyone else's—but the truth was, he thought about it a lot. Dicks with dicks. Cunts with cunts. A vacuum embracing another vacuum. A hole trying to fill a hole. In Duke's mind, to be any kind of homosexual was to admit that the world was empty.

Having heard from Ward Bond, Duke hoped that Pappy Ford would say something. To Duke's recollection, Ford had never said anything about anyone's homosexuality. And true to himself, Ford never spoke about Marlene's alleged affairs with women. Years earlier, though, over a poker game on his sailboat, Ford had stopped a conversation about faggotry by asking a question. "What would you say if it was your goddamn son? Or your brother?" The way he sounded, his anger at the thoughtlessness of their abstractions, ended the conversation.

The first and only time they went to Baja, Duke and Marlene were both between movies. In fact, they had borrowed the time for the trip from their publicity tour for *Seven Sinners*. Duke suspected she had other lovers, but that didn't matter so much. What she'd said about herself was true: she was a better swimmer than any woman he'd met, and after only four days on Baja, she'd become a better bodysurfer than he was.

Duke got tired more easily than he used to—he half suspected it was all the cigarettes he smoked—but Marlene never got tired. After a few hours of chasing waves, he allowed himself to return to the beach. He smoked and drank *cerveza* while he watched her slim body emerge and disappear among the darkening edges of the ocean.

By the time Marlene finally tired herself out and returned to the beach, Duke had made up his mind to ask her the question he'd always wanted to ask.

"People talk," he began slowly, "and I guess people talk to me because they think they know about us. You and other women, that's what it is. I want to know about you and other women. I want to know if it's true, how much of it is true."

Marlene had been clearing her ears of water. As she worked the towel into her head, she grudgingly turned her attention to Duke.

"Well," Marlene said. "This is it. This is the question that comes up, isn't it? I stupidly imagined that we could avoid this question. Why do you suddenly want to know?"

"I never felt like it before," Duke said.

"Is it a notion that disgusts you or appeals to you? We should get that settled first." Her voice became edgy the way it often did in the movies. He'd never heard it this way in life.

"It disgusts me," he said. "But *you* don't disgust me."

She smiled. "Will it disturb your manhood if I say 'yes'? Will it disturb your manhood if I say 'often'?"

Duke considered this. He hadn't prepared himself for her combative tone, but he should have expected it. "I didn't grow up with people who did things like that," he said. It came out more sadly than he had intended. "And it's never been part of my plans for myself."

"You grew up with lots of people who did things like that," Marlene said. "And we weren't talking about you. We were talking about me. Do you think it's going to make you queer if people find out that I'm queer?"

"That's not why I'm asking."

"Then why are you asking?"

"I just wanted to know." But suddenly he didn't have the heart for it. "Let's not talk about this," he said. "I'm getting tired of talking about this."

They returned to the cabana and made love.

The sex was good enough to cloak their discomfort for a while, but once they'd finished, he still wanted to ask her, *How is it different with a woman? Why do you have to do that?* So he asked her. He wasn't angry, but it must have sounded like anger. Her eyes narrowed. She asked him for a cigarette.

She said, "I don't have to tell you shit."

"Of course you don't," Duke said. "But I wanted to know, so I thought I would ask."

She always waited too long to light her cigarette. She held

her lighter between them as though it were a precious artifact. Whenever Duke thought he was getting close to her, there was always some actorly gesture that distanced them from each other. He took the lighter from her hand and lit her cigarette.

"I am a European free thinker." She flourished her cigarette as though she'd already given up hope of a good ending. "I go where my heart and my pussy tell me to go. They are like the magnets that give me direction. Often it has been that they take me toward a woman."

"That's bullshit."

"How would you know? You don't know what I feel. You have no idea what I feel." She flicked an ash into a paper cup toddling beside the cot. The ash sparkled and then sizzled in the drop of wine that was left at the bottom. She watched it. "Have *you* ever been with anyone who wasn't smaller and kinder and softer than you?"

"You certainly aren't any kinder."

"Are you afraid to answer the question?"

He was. It was a question no one had ever asked him. He searched his memory carefully to be certain he could answer honestly, and if he needed to lie, he could lie knowing that he was lying.

"No," he said. "But I don't see what that has to do with anything."

"It has to do with everything."

"I'm trying to understand," Duke said. "I've wanted to understand all along."

"You won't ever. You're not capable of it."

"Then I'll go fuck some pansy and come back and we can have this conversation."

"Why don't you do that?"

They patched things up. They agreed not to talk about it again. Having reached the frontier of their intimacy, they lacked the gumption to proceed. Over the next few months, during carefully planned weekends to Santa Barbara or Crestline or Joshua Tree, they continued to see each other. But it was never the same after Mexico.

And then Duke visited Pappy Ford's house. It was the end of spring, just as the hills above Hollywood were starting to get hot. They played bridge outside with Ford's wife and daughter, they swam in the pool with Ford's grandson, and then they retired to Ford's dark study, where they sat and talked and drank tequila. Ford had been thinking about making a movie based on a Eugene O'Neill play. After they'd discussed the plot, which concerned merchant seamen dodging U-boats in the English Channel, Ford laughed and said, "You still seeing that old German broad, what's her name?"

"You know what her name is, Pappy."

"She'll tell you she didn't screw Hitler, but I want you to know she did. I got that from Washington."

"What difference does it make?"

"She's a cabaret singer with a shtick," Ford said. "She's not an actress."

"I don't need her to be an actress."

"She isn't a wife, either," Ford said.

"I don't need her to be a wife."

"Then what the hell do you need her for?"

Duke smiled through the interrogation, but Ford was starting to get on his nerves. Why didn't he just come out and say it? *She's bad for you. She'll steal your strength. You can't afford to spend your life on such a powerful, heartless woman.* But Pappy just smiled, as though he were doing nothing more than making a good joke at Duke's expense. That was Ford's way. He'd been a great artist and a cranky bastard most of his life. He had a talent for provocation that was unmatched in the movie industry. It was essential to his method as a director.

Once Duke had started to understand Marlene in those terms, he couldn't stop. Once he'd seen her through Ford's eyes—as a powerful, dangerous woman—he couldn't stop seeing her that way, and this new vision infected all areas of his life. The attachment he'd sought with Marlene was the same attachment he'd sought with everyone—he'd wanted love, but also resistance. When it came down to it, he felt no more connection to his wife than he did to Marlene. Neither could he imagine what bound him to John Ford or his friends or his children or the American movie industry. He was more alone than he had ever been before. But he was starting to see the potential in loneliness.

As he prepared to move on with his career, he could look back on his younger self with amusement and pity. He had so much wanted connection, and now he saw connection as a liability. Loneliness, Duke thought, was freedom. Ford had tried to tell him, in his odd way, that there was no more room for delusions. If he wanted transcendence, he'd better roll up his sleeves and see what he could make of the earth he was standing on. A sexual adventure was one thing. The work of becoming a movie star was infinitely more difficult.

When he got the call from Ford to star in *The Long Voyage Home,* he knew that he couldn't afford Marlene anymore. It wasn't about her increasing disdain for him, nor was it about her age or her status in Hollywood. It was about all the ways he limited himself in her company. He couldn't love a woman like Marlene any more than he could star in a screwball comedy. He had to become *himself,* above all things, more completely than he had ever imagined possible. Ford was calling him toward a new way of seeing that thing called John Wayne.

The last time Duke saw Marlene alone, he was on his way to Mexico with the boys. He had finished filming *The Long Voyage Home,* and it looked as though America would soon be entering the war. He'd spend a few days in Ensenada with Ward Bond and Yakima Canutt, and then maybe they would take a plane to Cabo San Lucas, depending on how much time they had or how much fun they thought they could endure. He stopped by Marlene's house on his way toward San Diego.

He had intended to make love to her one last time, but first he needed to speak with her about something, anything. About God, for example, or about the freshness he felt deep down when he woke up early on location and was ready to perform before a camera. He wanted to tell her how he imagined he could see right through to heaven in the sharp Mexican light. How, hung over from a bad drunk and lying on the beach, he thought he saw honest-to-fucking-God cosmic figures dancing above him like a mural in an Indian restaurant. Beautiful voices. Horribly beautiful faces.

As he tried to say these things—they were in her house, a tired-looking European mansion—she plucked at the top button of his shirt and chided him that it wasn't nice to hide his throat from an admiring world. If he wasn't going to wear a tie, he needed to let his throat breathe. As she smoothed the skin over his Adam's apple and tugged another button from its hole, he thought that at least he could explain the feeling she'd given him just then.

He began by holding the hand that was trying to open his shirt. As her other hand reached up to finish the job, he held it, too.

"If you knew how much this made me feel," Duke said, "you'd think differently about everything."

"What's the matter? You don't want to feel?"

"We don't have a frame for this. I can't do it anymore without some . . . frame."

She shrugged off his hands and continued to unbutton his shirt. "You want to marry me, maybe?"

He shook his head. He wished that he could say yes. Marlene's delight in him seemed to increase.

"Tell me," she said.

"If I can't say anything to you, you've got to say something to me. Just one true thing about what we did together. I need to know that I wasn't alone."

She dropped her hands to her sides. She watched him carefully.

"Anything that's true," Duke said.

"The weight of your body on top of me. Smoking cigarettes together. All the stupid, stupid things you say about America the Beautiful. See, there's three things."

"Stop it."

"Well, how about this? I was nice to you at a time in your life when not everyone was nice to you."

"That's close."

"Thank you for saying so." Marlene smiled. "You want to make love to me one more time before you become too big a movie star for it?"

"I can't."

But when Duke reached Mexico—he met Ward and Yakima at a bar just over the border, and from there they drove to Ensenada—he still couldn't force the image of her face from his mind. Somewhere near Laguna Beach, he had passed the point where it was still pleasant to think about that last moment when she realized there was nothing, not even the greatest blowjob in the world, which could bring them together one more time. And then he was left with just her face, with all the time they'd spent together, which now seemed wasted. She was right—he was beginning to believe he would be a big star someday. Ford had always said he would. But, then again, Ford believed in angels and leprechauns and sometimes even the Democratic Party. Ford had also said he would give Duke a break someday, and indeed he had. He'd put Duke in *Stagecoach* and now *The Long Voyage Home,* and it looked as though things were going to be okay.

Ward and Yakima took out a boat almost as soon as they arrived, but Duke couldn't be persuaded to come along. Actually, they didn't try so hard. He just sat on the fishy verandah and counted his blessings. Now and again, the beach was crossed by aimless dogs and unwatched children. What kind of town was this where kids could wander near the water alone? He'd been neglecting his wife, but she would forgive him. He'd been neglecting his children, but they hadn't noticed yet. He brought home big pictures of himself, and that seemed to suit them as well as the real man would have. There were too many good ways to lose yourself in this world—he stretched his bad knee against a sun-heated bench—and he didn't have to count himself a genius because he'd stumbled over one of the more obvious.

STAGECOACH

1969

FRANK BARDEN WAS ON HIS KNEES CUTTING A CROWN MOLD- ING WHEN A HUGE BALD MAN ASKED IF CLAIRE WAS HOME. FRANK ALMOST RECOGNIZED THE VOICE, BUT IT WASN'T UNTIL HE GOT UP THAT HE REALIZED HE WAS STANDING TOE TO TOE WITH A BALD JOHN WAYNE. THAT'S WHAT HE THOUGHT, TOO: THIS MAN LOOKS JUST LIKE JOHN WAYNE EXCEPT HE'S BALD.

Because Claire wasn't home, Wayne ran out for some donuts and coffee. When he returned, Frank had just—once again—fucked up the miter on the crown molding for Milton's study. It was the fourth time since Wayne had left. Aside from Claire Trevor, Frank had never met a movie star before, and when he heard John Wayne's sneakers slapping across the patio toward the sliding glass door, he was crouching in the middle of the room beside his miter box and Skilsaw like a child among spent toys.

"What's the matter?" Wayne asked.

"I keep fucking up this miter, and I'm running out of crown molding to fuck it up on."

Wayne laughed and invited Frank to join him on Claire's patio beside the pool. From where they sat, they could hear boats and seabirds from Newport Bay.

"You shouldn't be so hard on yourself," Wayne said. "I broke your concentration."

Frank smiled cautiously. "It's been like this all day. It was like this before you came."

"Join the club," Wayne said. "This morning, I wouldn't know my fat ass from a pomegranate."

It was a consolation and Frank welcomed it. As Wayne pushed the open box of donuts toward him, Frank tried to imagine which ones Wayne would like so that he could pick something else. As he carefully pulled an Old Fashioned from the box and John Wayne sipped his coffee, Frank tried to explain. "There are some things where either God's with you or He isn't. All the skill in the world isn't going to get the miter on a crown molding right if you haven't got an angel on your shoulder."

Wayne nodded as though he understood. He said, "All I ever knew how to do was what other people told me. Lucky for me, I follow instructions *real* well."

"What are you talking about? You're a great actor."

"I'm just being honest. I know who I am."

"Right. You're the greatest actor in the world." Frank was still nervous, but it felt good to tell John Wayne the truth.

"Listen to me. I have focus. I work hard. I'm *not* a great actor."

"That sounds good," Frank said. "I don't buy it, but that sounds good."

"You think I'm just being humble?" Wayne set down his coffee. "Is that what you think?"

"No," Frank said. "I think you believe it, but you're wrong."

Wayne couldn't help but smile. "Take a look and see if there's a cruller in there, will you?"

Frank poked through the donuts. "No, you're wrong. You're just wrong. But there's a grain of truth in what you say." Frank handed Wayne the cruller.

"And what would that be?"

"Well," Frank said, "I would never tell anyone I work for, but I get scared every time I start a big job. I'm afraid someone's going to find out the truth about me."

"What's the truth?" Wayne said.

"Like what you said, that I'm just a worker, that I don't have what it takes to really make a mark."

"Jeez," Wayne said. "That's pretty good."

"You like that? You like what I said?"

"This cruller, I mean. You figure every Winchell's Donuts has got to be the same, but the one over here is better than the one that's near my house."

———

John Wayne had a small round table near the corner of his vast living room. From it, Frank could see the lawn, Newport Bay, and, beyond that, the Balboa Pavilion. Ordering a drink from Ernesto—Wayne's Mexican servant—Frank was already imagining ways to improve the building. When he was finished with Claire Trevor's house, he would begin on John Wayne's. Ernesto brought them drinks, and Frank accepted a barely diluted Canadian Club. Wayne drank his tequila, which Frank envied but hadn't asked for. Wayne was talking about how he'd come to California.

"My father was sick, and the doctor thought the Mojave Fucking Desert would bring back his lungs. After that didn't work out—my father wasn't a good farmer—we moved to Glendale. Once we got there, though, my parents started yelling at each other all the time. Later, they got divorced. I was a tough, straight-arrow kid from Iowa, and this wasn't the best thing that could happen to me. I started getting into fistfights because my real name was Marion. I got good at fistfights."

"Your name was Marion?"

"Marion Michael Morrison. Why are you smiling?"

"My name was—I mean, *is*—Francis Michael Barden."

"Is that why you're smiling?"

"Yeah. I got good at fistfights, too."

Wayne laughed. They both laughed. Laughter was like a big balloon over their conversation. Frank, becoming enthusiastic with the bourbon, offered his own memory:

"I beat up a guy in a bar once. I don't remember who he was. I think he was a reporter, some kind of writer, maybe. Anyway, they locked both of us up, and somehow the word got around the corner to my father. When they brought me to the judge, my pop was in the courtroom, looking at me like I'd killed all his hope for the future."

Wayne scratched the fuzzy back of his head. His bare forearm was old and great like a tree. He narrowed his eyes and smiled. "What did he know about fighting? Did he know anything about fighting?"

"He was a fighter," Frank said. "I'd seen him fight when I was a kid. He was wiry, not nearly as big as I am. But all those old Irish guys learned to fight. That was part of the deal."

Wayne let his eyes open and his smile disappeared. "You're still thinking about this after all these years?"

"Yeah, I guess so."

"Why?"

"I don't know. You said something about your father and I wanted to say something about mine. I thought we were having a conversation."

"What would you say if it were your son and you were your dad watching him?"

"I'd be proud. He's been such a pansy up till now."

"Well, there you have it. You have no reason to be ashamed." Wayne shifted in his seat, in the way that a large man will, as though nothing will ever be big enough for him.

"I didn't say I was ashamed. I was just telling you a story."

"Okay, okay. But tell me this: If you would feel that way about your son, what makes you think your father would feel differently about you?"

"Because he told me so later. He said he was ashamed of me and I'd behaved like a peasant."

"Oh."

"But, I mean, you would have been right if he hadn't said that."

As they talked, a lonely cloud passed between John Wayne's house and the sun. The house went dark for a moment and then burst again with light. Frank was beginning to feel the booze.

"Oh, I'm so fucking sick and tired of all this," Wayne said.

Frank was almost startled out of his drunkenness. "What? What do you mean?"

"I mean . . . look at me. I'm sixty-two years old, blowing cigar smoke out of one lung, *sipping* tequila. Hell, I don't even kiss girls *on the screen* anymore. Biggest fucking actor in the world! Let me tell you, I've got scars all up and down my body. I'm a fucking mess!"

"I think you're doing pretty well," Frank said. "I mean, you've helped me a lot."

"I've *helped* you?" Wayne said. "What do you mean I've *helped* you."

"Well, it was just . . . you told me about . . ."

"So, you mean I'm like a fucking *buddy* to you? Is that what you mean? Jesus Christ! Jesus Fucking Christ!"

"That's not . . ."

"Doesn't this mean anything to you? Doesn't the fact that I'm sitting here getting drunk mean anything to you? Am I sitting here for your fucking education? Are you here to fucking learn something? What about me? Are you going to be *my* buddy?"

"Now hold on a fucking minute," Frank said. "I don't need you for a fucking *buddy*, all right?"

"That's better. I don't need any more fucking buddies."

"Besides, I hardly know you. You could turn out to be a real asshole."

"Oh, don't worry about that. You'd be doing *fucking great* if I was your buddy. Don't worry about that."

Wayne finished his tequila, and Frank wondered what it tasted like. He watched the golden liquid disappear down Wayne's throat, and his own glass of scotch seemed less appealing. He threw it back anyway. Immediately, Wayne called down the hallway for another drink, and Frank said he wouldn't mind trying some of Wayne's tequila. He felt mysteriously happy when Wayne instructed Ernesto to just leave the whole goddamn bottle on the table between them.

Duke decided that they should take a drive. Certain things couldn't be said in living rooms or on patios. They needed to be said in cars or trucks or bars. He asked Frank to drive them to a place in Laguna Beach called The White House. He told Frank not to call him "Mr. Wayne" anymore—his name was "Duke." They took Frank's brand-new Chevy pickup.

As Frank and Duke lumbered through the door toward seats beside an antiqued mirror, the sharp light from Pacific Coast Highway filled the bar. Men still crisp from the workday drank here and there. Couples ate late lunch or early dinner. A young woman approached them. Her hair was brown turning to sunny gold. Like tequila, Frank thought.

"What can I do for you gentlemen?"

Duke asked for her name even though she was sporting a laminate nameplate on her frilly blouse.

"Tracy," she said.

"Tracy, my friend Frank and I would like shots of Conmemorativo and a couple of beers. Can you do that for us?"

"Yes, sir." Tracy retreated from the table. Frank felt better than he had all afternoon. He felt powerful within himself in a way that didn't depend on John Wayne's presence but was infinitely expanded by it. He was glad to be with John Wayne, but he would have been glad to be with anyone. He felt like a movie star himself.

Wayne removed his trucker's cap and ran his large hand over the dome of his scalp. "God help you if you ever go bald, Frank Barden."

"You look good." Frank smiled. "You look like John Wayne."

Duke laughed. "That's right," he said. "I do look like John Wayne, don't I?"

"I should be scared shitless, sitting here drinking with you," Frank said, "but I'm not afraid at all. I *like* drinking with you."

"I'll take that as a compliment."

"It *is* a compliment. Of course it's a fucking compliment."

The waitress returned with their drinks and a bowl of nuts. Frank couldn't remember if they'd asked for any. She was a tall, thin girl like Lillian, although about ten years younger and even more self-contained. He figured her for a college student or, like so many of them, a *former* college student. Frank must have been staring at her because when she left the table, Duke stared at Frank.

"What?" Frank said. "Was I drooling or something?"

Duke smiled. "Tell me about your wife."

"You don't want to hear about my wife," Frank said. "You just want to make me feel guilty about the waitress."

"No, I want to hear about your wife. She's from the Bronx, too?"

"Yeah."

"Tell me about her."

"Like that one," Frank pointed, "but a little older. Tall, slim, darker hair."

"I don't care about her goddamn figure. I mean, what's she like?"

It was a question Frank didn't really know how to answer. The idea that he might explain Lillian seemed absurd.

"Smarter than I am," Frank said. "Tough. It was her idea to move to California. I wouldn't have figured that out. She does all the bookkeeping for my business. Helps me come up with a business plan every few years. She's finishing her degree, too. Reads everything. Makes me feel stupid *almost all the time.*"

"Do you like her?"

"She's my wife." Frank laughed. "I love her."

"Yeah, but do you *like* her?"

"I like her."

Duke lost his smile. He stared off toward a wedge of sunlight crossing the tile floor. He looked over the room as though he'd lost something. Without facing Frank, he spoke again. "Is she *happy?*"

"Sometimes she's happy."

"What the fuck does *that* mean?"

"She thinks I've put her in a cage," Frank said. "I'm more scared of her than I am of you."

Duke's eyes returned to Frank. "Scared?" he said.

"Scared she's going to leave me."

Duke seemed to rally himself around the idea of Frank's fear. He straightened up his chair and stared thoughtfully at the small table between them. He scratched his left hand and then placed both hands in his lap.

"It's important to work hard," Duke said. "No one believes me, but I think that helps a marriage more than anything. Work hard, make lots of money, give her most of it."

"I do those things," Frank said.

"Then make more money," Duke said. "Just keep working. Take on something that you're sure will kill you. Hell, I'll even give you the money to kill yourself with. I wish I'd known that much when I was thirty-five. I wouldn't have wasted so much time. When I was fifty, I knew better. I was working three months after they took out my lung."

"I don't know," Frank said.

"What don't you know?"

"You think that'll do it?"

"Sure that'll do it. Why the fuck wouldn't that do it?"

"Where's *your* wife today?"

"My wife? I don't know where she is. I'm out of the house before she wakes up."

Frank looked toward Tracy, who was perched beside the bar, and he tried to imagine another way. He hadn't been very thoughtful about the possibilities besides Lillian. She'd been hard to get and he was lucky to have her. He watched himself in the mirror beside Tracy. A little heavier than he'd been in the Marine Corps, but still good-looking. He watched himself and then he watched Tracy. She wasn't too young for him, he thought. She wasn't too pretty.

"Do you think she knows you're John Wayne?" Frank asked.

"Yeah." Duke looked toward Tracy. "I guess so."

"She doesn't act like she knows."

As though she'd heard him, Tracy returned to the table. She walked more slowly than before, or it seemed that way to Frank, who watched her fiercely as she crossed the checkerboard tiled floor.

"Almost finished? Need some more?" Less courtly than before, she seemed to recognize Frank's fierceness.

"I guess we need two more," Duke said. "And some more of those nuts would be good."

Frank never stopped watching her face. She was beginning to show age around her eyes, even though she was still so young. She never once looked at Frank.

"What kind of beer is this?" Frank asked.

She smiled at him and then her smile went sour. "You know, I really don't remember. It's tap. I'm new here. Let me go check."

"That's okay," Frank said. "I was just wondering."

She smiled again at Frank, but it seemed like a dishonest smile. She put a lot of teeth into it. "It's no trouble," she said.

As she returned to the bar, Frank said, "There's something strange about her."

"What's that?"

"I don't know. There's just something I don't like. She's got some kind of attitude. You know what I mean?"

Duke wrinkled his forehead and looked back toward the bar. He narrowed his eyes as though it was difficult to see. "I'll have to trust you on that one," he said. "I promise I won't like her any more than I have to until she gets back with our drinks."

"I think she feels superior somehow," Frank said. "I think she's looking down on us. I don't know why that is. I'm just picking up on it."

"You could be right," Duke said. "Maybe she's a college student. Contempt seems to come with the territory."

When Tracy returned with their drinks and a fresh bowl of nuts, Frank was certain she was playing a game with them. How could she not recognize John Wayne? He spent a moment considering that it might be politeness until he was certain again that it wasn't. He saw no fear or reverence or concern in her face. She looked like the women he saw on television, so sure of themselves and the joke they were playing on the men around them. He couldn't keep silent. He had to do something.

"It's Coors," Tracy said.

"This is Mr. Wayne," Frank said. "May I introduce you to Mr. Wayne? My name's Frank."

"Hello, Mr. Wayne. Hello, Frank. Are you gentlemen off from work today?"

"We don't work as hard as we used to," Duke said. "Besides, it's Friday afternoon. Don't we get to cut out a little early on Friday afternoon?"

"Of course." She smiled. "You let me know if you need anything else."

As Tracy walked away, Frank followed her with his eyes. She was a bigger girl than he'd thought. Not quite as tall as Lillian, but larger in the ass. Her legs were stronger, too. Bold, well-defined calves. He was grateful she was wearing a skirt. So many of them didn't wear skirts anymore.

"She doesn't know who you are," Frank said.

"It happens. Believe it or not, some people don't even watch television, let alone the movies."

"But isn't it strange?"

"Yes, it's odd."

"God, it's just fucking strange." Frank felt cheated. He looked around the bar, and, inconceivably, no one was looking back at him. He watched Duke to make sure he wasn't some kind of impostor.

"What?"

"Nothing," Frank said.

"You're worried."

"What should I be worried about?"

"Because no one recognizes me."

"No way."

"Trust me. This happens all the fucking time."

"But how can that happen? You shouldn't be able to walk into a bar and have no one recognize you. You're John Fucking Wayne."

"Frank, let me ask you something. If you're not too busy worrying about the fucking waitress."

"Sure."

"Call me Duke."

"Sure, Duke."

"Did you ever see *Stagecoach?*"

"Jeez, I must have seen *Stagecoach* seventeen times. I think I saw it on TV a few months ago."

"You know that part where the Ringo Kid almost gets talked into running away by Dallas?"

"That was Claire. Claire played that part."

"That's right."

"Yeah, I remember. She talks him into leaving that ranch and he starts to leave, but before he can get away from the marshal, he sees smoke signals and realizes that the stagecoach is in trouble and he can't do it."

"I fucking *hated* that."

"What do you mean?"

"I just fucking *hated* it. Didn't want to do it. I thought a guy like Ringo would never run away, even for a woman. If we'd been doing it ten years later, I would have never let that scene get through."

"Did you say anything about it?"

"I couldn't. Ford was directing, and I was too chickenshit to say anything to Ford."

Frank didn't understand. He was trying to connect this story to Tracy, but he couldn't do it.

"And you know what else I hated?"

"What?"

"I hated dying. But the films in which I died always did better. That was a funny thing."

"How many times did you die?"

"I don't know. Seven or eight times. Those films always did *real* good."

Frank thought about all that Wayne had said, which was becoming difficult. By now, he was close to *truly* drunk.

"Tell me something," Frank said. "What the hell does this have to do with the waitress?"

"This has nothing to do with the waitress."

"Oh."

"Can I tell you one more thing, though?"

"Sure, Duke."

"On *Stagecoach,* Ford fucking tortured me from start to finish. First day of shooting and he starts riding me about how I'm washing my hands. I'm off to the side of the frame—just a little fucking *dot* on the screen—and he stops the whole fucking production. 'Duke, stop washing your hands like a fucking faggot.' Oh, it was horrible. So, the next take, I scrub and slap and strain my arms, and again he cuts the camera. 'Jesus, Duke, if you can't even wash your hands *like a man,* how am I going to use you in the rest of the picture?' Oh Christ, it was even worse the second time! Finally, little Timmy Holt, who played a cavalry officer, walked over and said, 'Pappy, don't be so hard on Duke. He's doing the best he can.' "

Duke pitched sideways in his chair, laughing harder than

Frank had seen him in their short time as drinking partners. His laugh was bigger than the room, and people turned from their drinking and eating to watch him laugh.

"Don't you get it?" Duke asked.

"Get what?"

"Ford was welcoming me to the world of men. He got the crew to stick up for me. From that day on, they treated me like I was their friend."

Frank pondered this. The story seemed appropriate in a way that he couldn't quite grasp.

"Why were you thinking about this?" Frank asked. "What made you think about this?"

"Hell, I don't know." Duke smiled. "Tell me about your wife again."

"Why the hell are you so interested in my wife?"

"Because I'd rather talk about your wife than my wife. I'm so sick and tired of talking about my wife. Is that all right with you?"

Frank relented. Surrender to Duke's will felt like a blessing.

"She's starting to lose her accent," Frank said. "She's starting to sound like California. I don't even know what California sounds like, but she doesn't sound like New York anymore."

"There's nothing wrong with school, Frank."

"Did I say there was anything wrong with school?"

"No, but you seemed a little worried about your wife getting a degree. Hell, I almost got a degree once. From USC."

"You went to USC?"

"Played football even."

"That's good, isn't it?"

"That's very good. That's as good as it gets."

"I'm sorry I got mad at you."

"That's all right. Just don't hit me or I'll have to kill you."

"Would you really kill me?" Frank asked. "I'm the best friend you've got."

"That's *why* I'd kill you."

Wayne laughed, again much harder than he needed to. Tracy watched him from the bar.

"So tell me about your wife," Duke said. "This is the last fucking time I'm going to ask you."

"Why are we talking about my wife? Why not talk about *your* wife?"

"Because I don't fucking want to talk about my goddamn wife," Duke sputtered.

"Why don't we talk about the waitress?"

"Because I don't want to talk about the cocksucking waitress."

"She's a fucking whore if she doesn't know who you are."

"Frank, just tell me," Duke said. "I'm not going to ask you again."

Frank smiled. Duke was drunk and angry, and somehow that pleased him. He leaned forward and whispered into Duke's ear. "My wife's going to leave me," Frank said. "Probably soon."

The stretch of Pacific Coast Highway between Laguna Beach and Newport Beach was undeveloped. There was the road and the roadside fruit and vegetable shacks, but beyond that, there was nothing but the Coast Range, like a brown shelf set just above the Pacific Ocean. By the time they hit the road, the haze had completely burned off, and the ocean was too blue and the hills were too brown and the road was stark like a black snake in the sand.

Frank sited the road over the great hood of his Chevy. He drove too fast.

"It's not what I expected to be doing on a Friday afternoon, getting drunk with John Wayne."

"John *Fucking* Wayne," Duke corrected him.

"John *Fucking* Wayne, I'm sorry. Why don't we bulldoze the whole fucking coast and make an amusement park. We'll call it JOHN FUCKING WAYNE LAND. Walt Fucking Disney ain't . . ."

"There's something I have to tell you," Duke interrupted him. He looked so big there in the passenger seat. Frank was sure he'd never seen anyone so big in his brand-new truck. Wayne tugged at the brim of his trucker's cap. "It's something I was thinking about before that I wanted to tell you." Wayne coughed and rolled down the window to spit. "I wanted to tell you that the world is full of sons of bitches."

"And whores," Frank added.

"And whores."

"I know that," Frank said solemnly.

"But some of those sons of bitches are going to love you and you're going to love them back. And some of those whores are going to be closer to you than your own breath. And you've got to be able to tell the difference between the ones you love and the ones you don't love. It doesn't make a goddamn bit of difference to the world, but it makes all the difference to you. I'm going to be one of the bastards that loves you, and you've gotta know the difference between me and someone else."

"How do I tell if you're you?"

Wayne pondered this as though it was an important question. He stared out the window as an electric-blue Corvette passed them on the left. Too close, much too fucking close. Frank gave him the finger.

"You'll know I'm me because I'm the one who loves you."

This satisfied Frank. They drove the rest of the way to Newport Beach in silence.

John Wayne's Station Wagon

1971

Frank's rented tuxedo was on a chair near the end of the bed. Lillian couldn't remember sleeping with him last night. She wondered where he was.

She retrieved her nightgown from the master bathroom and cautiously entered the rest of the house. Sometimes, when she woke up, she felt as though she were putting on her home with her clothes. This was the house Frank had built on spec—they were never supposed to move into it, they had never wanted to live in a town like Orange. As much as she had tried to dress it up and make it over, it still had the provisional quality of a tract home. This morning, she wanted to take an ax to every piece of furniture, dig up the floors, and burn it down.

She quietly opened the front door and entered the day. When she reached the driveway, she saw that her house was surrounded by huge vehicles—Phil and Arlene's camper was in front of her, Frank's Buick was beside her, and John Wayne's green station wagon was parked at the curb near the end of the lawn. Her son Danny was sitting on the front seat, his head bobbing in and out of view as he inspected the dashboard. Frank was behind her in the garage. She heard him setting down something heavy on the workbench.

Frank moved toward her.

"The roof's been extended," Frank said. "He loves station wagons, but I guess they're not quite big enough for him."

"I see."

"Listen, Lillian, I'm so sorry. I remember it all. Nothing like that's going to ever happen again."

Lillian turned toward him. "It won't ever happen again because I'm going to make sure it doesn't happen again."

"What do you mean, Lil?"

"Fuck you, Frank."

Just then, Arlene and Phil emerged from their camper. Arlene stepped warily onto Milford Road, as though she were afraid it had disappeared during the night. Phil stepped out jauntily after her.

"Did you guys sleep well?" Lillian shouted.

"Just fine," Phil announced. "I don't even know why we keep the house, it's so comfortable in there."

Arlene made a face to convey that she didn't agree. Lillian laughed.

"You guys want to wait for me inside?" Lillian said. "And we can fix some breakfast?"

Arlene and Phil marched toward the house. Danny now watched his parents through the windshield, the green tinting darkening his face.

"Lillian," Frank said. "Jesus, Lillian."

"I'm going to go in and fix breakfast for our friends."

She followed them inside. Arlene and Phil were seated on stools across the counter from Lillian's stove.

"God, I'm so hungry," Phil said. "Drinking always makes me hungry."

"Are you okay?" Arlene asked Lillian.

"I'm fine. Scrambled eggs and bacon? Toast?" Lillian's hands were trembling as she reached for the refrigerator door.

Lillian's daughter Alice shuffled through the dining room toward the kitchen. She was imitating her little brother, who ambled awkwardly beside her, attached to her hand.

"I was afraid you weren't ever going to get home," Alice said. "I waited and waited and then I fell asleep."

"Come over here, sweetheart," Arlene said.

Alice reluctantly surrendered her attachment to her brother Chris, who floated like a spaceman before he dropped happily to the ground.

Alice kissed Arlene, but she kept her eyes on Lillian.

"What were you doing while you waited?" Arlene asked. "Were you reading?"

"I can't read in the dark."

"Your mother never taught you how to read in the dark?"
Alice's eyes narrowed in dismay.

Lillian smiled tightly and began to concentrate on breakfast.
She set the kettle to boil for instant coffee as Phil hauled Chris
from the floor and set him ceremoniously on his lap. She pulled
down a skillet and stood for a long moment watching it, touching
the handle as though she were amazed by its substance.

When the phone rang, Lillian left the skillet clattering on the
range. She reached the wall before the phone could ring again.

It was John Wayne. "Lillian, we made a little mistake last
night. Frank drove home the Oldsmobile, and it's full of *Christmas
presents*. I need those back here as soon as possible. I'm sorry—I
should have given him another car."

"He'll get them back there this morning."

"Did you have a nice time last night?"

"Sure."

"I'm glad. It was good to see you. So, Frank can take care of
that?"

"Sure."

"Great, great."

When she returned the phone to the wall, Phil and Arlene
and even Alice seemed to know that something important had
happened. John Wayne's station wagon was full of Christmas
presents. Why was that important?

"That was Duke Wayne. He needs his car back."

Lillian walked through the kitchen into the garage. Frank and
Danny were already standing behind the huge green station
wagon, staring at the colorful boxes and wrapped packages, each a
different size and shape.

She stood beside her husband and son, but refused to share

their wonder. "Wayne wants you to bring them back," Lillian said, and then she turned toward the house.

"I need someone to go with me," Frank said.

Lillian turned around. She wanted to scream at Frank, but the first thing she saw was Danny's face.

"Call Jimmy."

"Jimmy's with his girlfriend in Palm Desert."

"Go across the street and ask Randy."

Frank looked at the house across the street and quietly said, "I'm not driving to Newport Beach with fucking Randy."

"Frank, I don't care."

"I'll go with you," Danny offered.

"You can go," Lillian explained, "but that doesn't solve the problem. Your father needs someone to drive him back."

Danny seemed relieved that his participation was not essential.

"Listen," Lillian said, "Arlene and Phil need to eat. Duke can wait until after breakfast. Phil will go with you."

"Why don't we wait until after breakfast," Frank asked, "and then *you* can go with me?"

"Because I don't want to go with you. Anywhere."

Danny winced, but Lillian walked away toward the house. After a moment, Frank and Danny followed her.

Once inside, Lillian stood before the beginnings of her breakfast: a frying pan lying off-center on her radar range. Arlene had made coffee, which she handed to Lillian and Frank. Alice abandoned the room with her baby brother in tow, which left four people staring at Lillian. She addressed Frank in a cold attempt to prevent him from speaking.

"I'm fixing breakfast. I'll be done when I'm done. Don't wait around on me if you need to go now."

Lillian retrieved a package of bacon and several eggs from the refrigerator, and then she fumbled with both bacon and eggs until Arlene slid off her stool and took everything from Lillian's hands. Without any more protest than she could show in her pained eyes, Lillian sat down on the stool next to Phil.

The phone rang again. Frank stood in the middle of the kitchen, unwilling or unable to move. Lillian reached awkwardly toward the wall. It was John Wayne's secretary, Pat Stacy.

"Hi, Lillian, it's Pat. Mr. Wayne made another mistake. He needs the station wagon right now. Can someone drive it over *right now?*"

"Hold on a second, Pat." Lillian covered the receiver and addressed Frank.

"They need the car now."

Frank watched her before he said, "Will you come with me?"

"We've got guests," she said, but she looked at Phil as she said it. She stared at him.

Arlene picked up the cue. "Phil's been looking for an excuse to see the *Wild Goose* one more time. Phil will go with you."

Both Frank and Phil seemed disappointed.

"That'd be great," Phil said. "Maybe Duke will change his mind and give me a job on his next picture."

Frank said nothing. Lillian dug through her purse and came up with a set of keys, which she placed in Phil's hand. "Follow Frank in the Buick. That camper makes me nervous. Danny, you go with them."

Frank continued to watch her without offering anything. Danny watched the floor. Phil smiled at his wife, and then at Lillian, who did not smile back.

When the children had been fed and the dishes cleared, Arlene suggested a walk. According to her, she had become accustomed to the great open spaces near Lompoc, and she felt stifled by the more conventional suburbs of Orange County. Lillian recognized an attempt to be a good friend.

Lillian's house was at a dead end beside a field where a crop of new houses had just been framed. Beyond the end of Milford Road, streets had been graded but no cement had been poured. Lillian had never walked through the tract before.

They set out down the dirt road that turned out and away from Lillian's house. Every new home would be a one-story like her own, and every fourth house would be exactly the same, except for paint and trim, which would come later. Arlene was fascinated with the half-built homes.

"Now, what's the deal with something like this? Would John Wayne give Frank the money to build a tract? Is this the kind of thing that Frank wants to get into?"

They had turned toward the Santiago Creek, which was really just a big ditch for flood control, pouring down from the Santa Ana Mountains toward the Santa Ana River. Last spring, it had been so full that it had almost washed away Lillian's home. These new houses were built right up to its edge.

"I have a feeling," Lillian said, "that this is a little too complicated for Duke. Apartment buildings are mostly what they're talking about. Keep it for a couple of years, enjoy all the tax advantages, sell it. I think that's much simpler."

Lillian noticed herself getting interested in her husband again. It was insidious the way his problems had become her problems, his opportunities her opportunities. And it saddened her, the thought that she might no longer file his tax returns.

"Duke just wants to give him the money and have a problem-free real estate investment," Arlene said. "I can understand that. Frank's job is to make it as easy on him as possible."

"Yes," Lillian said. "That's it."

As they approached the flood-control channel—the Santiago Creek—Lillian could feel her insides rising to the memory of last spring's deluge. The children had been taken out of school, the area evacuated, and for a moment, it had looked as though their houses would be flooded in order to save a reservoir somewhere up in the mountains—a reservoir Lillian had never seen, never even *heard* of. She looked over the edge of the ditch and saw only a muddy trickle sixty feet below, winding through weeds and broken bicycles and incongruous stands of bamboo.

"You know what I'm thinking of?" Arlene asked.

"No."

"I'm thinking of the famous people I'd like to invest money in your apartment buildings."

"Oh, Jesus."

"What? You don't want me to tell you?"

"Sure, but tell me about it on the way home. This ridiculous creek bothers me even when it's empty."

As they turned away and started toward home, the sky above them was dissolving into blue. Near Christmas was the most beautiful time in Southern California. The sky was clear like the sky above her childhood. There was no smog on days like this, and the cool air made her feel awake. More than awake—alive.

The unfinished street was a little lower than her house, and when Lillian looked up toward Milford Road, she saw her daughter walking toward them. A small fear leapt in her chest before she could remind herself that she was doing nothing wrong.

Alice proceeded toward them with awesome concentration. She had changed from her pajamas into a playsuit.

"Where's your little brother?" Lillian asked.

"He's watching TV. A man called."

"What was the man's name?"

"He didn't say. He wanted to talk to you. I told him that you'd be right back."

"Did you recognize his voice?"

"No."

Lillian knew who it was. She could predict John Wayne's behavior by imagining a smarter, stronger Frank with more tolerance for alcohol. John Wayne was a Hollywood blowup of her husband. Better in some ways, but still annoying.

"Alice," Lillian said, "why don't you go make sure Chris stays out of trouble? Will you do that for me, sweetheart?"

"Where's Daddy?"

"Daddy had to drive to Newport Beach to return Mr. Wayne's car."

"Why couldn't Mr. Wayne come *here* to get his car?"

"Because that's not the way it works, sweetheart. When you borrow something, it's your job to return it."

"Mr. Wayne was the one who called."

"Thanks for telling me that, Alice. Why didn't you tell me that before?"

"You just reminded me of what he sounded like."

"Alice, go home and take care of your little brother the way I asked you to."

While Alice walked ahead of them, Arlene took greater notice of Lillian; she studied her with an intensity that Lillian could feel.

"Don't look at me that way, please."

"How was I looking at you?" Arlene asked.

"You want to know if something's wrong. Yes, something's wrong. You know as well as I do what's wrong."

"I'm *sorry.*"

"I don't know whether I'm going to divorce him, but it really feels like I'm going to divorce him."

Arlene looked over Lillian's shoulder toward Alice, who was trudging back toward the house. "Think hard," she said.

"What does *that* mean?"

"I don't know. It just seems like something someone should say."

Arlene bent down to recover a short piece of two-by-four with a long, jagged nail in its head. She threw it off the road toward what would one day be a sidewalk. "Another thing I'm supposed to say—oh, the hell with it, I'm not going to say it."

"Doesn't he seem like an asshole to you? Didn't he seem like an asshole last night?"

"I love Frank."

"And he's worse this morning. He's pathetic."

"I'm supposed to say that he's a good provider. You've got good kids and you've got a nice home and you should think about all those things because they're important. Not everyone can give you those things. Not everyone would want to."

"This isn't about that Michael character," Lillian said. "This has nothing to do with that Michael character."

Arlene looked as though she'd been caught snooping. She turned away and took a last look at the unfinished homes.

"I know that," she said.

As soon as they walked in the door, the phone rang. Arlene crossed the kitchen and carefully lifted the receiver off the wall.

"Hello? No, this is Arlene. Hi. Yes, she's right here. Yes, I had a wonderful time, thank you." Arlene handed the phone to Lillian, who accepted it as though bad news was about to find her. Arlene sat down without taking her eyes off Lillian's face.

"Yes. Yes, he left here an hour ago. Yeah, he should have been there by now. I'm sorry, I'm sure he'll be there soon. No problem. Absolutely. Bye."

Arlene couldn't help smiling. "Frank's not there yet."

"Yeah."

"Phil will keep him out of trouble."

"I doubt that. I'm worried about Danny." Lillian stood away from the counter and tried to rally herself. Arlene waited.

"No, it's not good. He's drinking somewhere, and he's not letting Phil or Danny get him home."

"Where does he drink down there?"

"I don't know. I bet Jimmy knows."

She called Frank's brother Jimmy, who she guessed would be home. Palm Desert sounded too ambitious for a heroin addict who liked the inside of his own apartment better than most places. He answered after ten rings.

"Jimmy, it's Lil."

"Yeah. Hi, Lil. Why are you calling me so early?"

"Listen, Frank's off somewhere and he's got John Wayne's car. Danny's with him and our friend Phil, and I'm a little worried. He left here about an hour ago, and he hasn't showed up at Wayne's house yet."

She heard the receiver change hands, and Jimmy waited too long to respond. Breathing heavily, he said, "Lil, what do you want me to do?"

"I want you to find him and get the car over to Duke's house and then get Danny back here."

The background disappeared as Jimmy covered the receiver. He spoke to someone else in the room. When he returned, there was a rush of complicated noise.

"I can't go right now. I have things to do."

"Jimmy, what the fuck are you doing that you can't help me?"

"Calm down, darling. I'm *going* to help you. I just can't drive over to Newport Beach. I'll come over to the house later. Do you have a pencil?"

"Yes, I have a fucking pencil."

"There's a place off Newport Boulevard—I think it's on Esplanade—called The Lighthouse. It's going to be there or at a place called Honey, I'm Home, which is on Harbor. If he's not at either of those places, maybe he went to The Rusty Pelican. Sometimes he likes to have lunch at The Rusty Pelican."

When Frank worked closer to home, she had her own map of where he might be. She wrote down all three names, but she put a box around The Rusty Pelican, which sounded like the only place he could bring Danny.

"Is that it?"

"If it's not one of those, maybe I can think of somewhere else. Call me if it's not one of those places. I'll be here until I come over to the house. Hey, how was the party?"

Lillian hung up the phone.

"What is it?" Arlene asked.

"I've got to go find him."

"What's the matter with Jimmy?"

"He needs to screw his girlfriend a few more times."

Arlene placed her hands on the table and accepted Lillian's fury.

"I'm sorry," Lillian said. "I'm not mad at you."

"I know you're not."

"It's just that he's such trash. They're all such trash. I look at my kids and I just hope that none of them grow up to be . . . trash." Lillian cried for the first time that morning. Her grief came over her with shuddering pain.

"Oh, honey." Arlene stood beside her at the kitchen counter. Arlene was an awkward woman who couldn't help but overwhelm her friend. As she felt Arlene closing around her, Lillian regained control. She stood up and gently opened Arlene's arms.

"I'm okay. I'm going to be okay. Can you watch the kids?"

The Newport Freeway was empty except for families on outings and working men in pickups. She felt conspicuous, alone in her red Dodge Dart. The sky continued blue until she reached the frontier between Irvine and Costa Mesa, where the coastal fog made the horizon look like a stiff white sheet of paper. She couldn't imagine anything beyond it but the kind of death that borrowed its terror from nothingness: falling from an airplane, drowning in a sea, smothering in a vast unpunctuated darkness.

She passed both Esplanade and Harbor and didn't turn off Newport until she'd reached Pacific Coast Highway. The Rusty Pelican was a carefully weathered copper-colored box on the harbor side of the road. In spite of its facade, it still seemed unfinished, as though the builders, in their zeal for an authentic seafaring surface, had forgotten to put a restaurant behind all the antique paint.

Both cars were in the parking lot, but not many others. She parked beside John Wayne's station wagon and waited for a few minutes with the sharp sense that she was about to repeat herself. For the thousandth time, she was going to stand between Frank and his drinking.

Lillian turned to look at the Christmas presents, which were just visible through the window. They were so many and various. She could recognize at least five different wrappings, and the frilly doodads that sparkled on top must have been the work of professionals. Maybe the presents were fabulously expensive and couldn't be replaced. Lillian couldn't imagine buying something that couldn't be replaced, but maybe John Wayne could. There were many things in the world a rich person could buy that no one would ever be able to have again. The thought of something that precious made Lillian afraid for herself and the world in which such things were possible.

As she sat in her Dodge, watching the presents, a car quietly snuck up behind her and *smacked* her rear bumper with enough force to jolt Lillian into screaming. It was her brother-in-law Jimmy with an embarrassed-looking blonde beside him. Jimmy was grinning extravagantly, his hands choked up on the steering wheel of his old fin-tailed Cadillac, his drug addict's eyes pegged to Lillian's fear. Lillian got out of her car and walked around to him.

"Just a kiss," he said. "Don't worry about it."

"You scared the shit out of me, Jimmy."

"I felt guilty, so I thought I'd come help you."

Lillian tried not to see the blonde, who sat too close beside Jimmy, but she looked like the kind of woman Jimmy favored:

pretty, but damaged. Jimmy himself could be a handsome man, but he was also damaged.

"Lil, this is Barbara."

Barbara started to extend her hand, but Lillian returned her attention to Jimmy.

"If you'd told me you were coming, I could have stayed home and watched the kids."

"I figured he was probably here," Jimmy said. "I had to think about it for a minute."

Barbara drew herself the smallest bit away. Lillian didn't like the look in Jimmy's eyes.

"Did he call you?" she asked.

"Yeah, he called me."

"Why didn't he take the station wagon back? Did he tell you that?"

"He didn't say anything about the station wagon. He said he wanted me to come down because he had to tell me something and maybe later we'd go see Duke."

"How drunk was he?"

"He was working on it."

"Oh, Jesus Christ."

Jimmy led her through the parking lot toward the front door. The Rusty Pelican was too dark. A waterfront restaurant, it was lit like a cave in order to avail itself of the quaint scenery just outside. Lillian's anxiety bloomed as she followed Jimmy and Barbara past the hostess stand toward the only bright table in the dining room, which was populated by her husband and son and Phil.

"There are too many fucking wonderful things in this area," Frank spoke to the table. "You can live like a king here. I don't understand why you want to live like a peasant somewhere else."

"I like Lompoc," Phil said.

Frank saw Jimmy and smiled. But the happy expectation that his party would be enlarged soon gave way as he saw Lillian. He started to stand from the table, and then, thinking better of himself, he sat down.

"Look at that bitch. Did you come all this way to rescue the Christmas presents? You care more about the fucking Christmas presents than you do about me."

Lillian remembered why she was there. She checked her son's face for the trouble she knew she'd find, but he was completely preoccupied with his father.

John Wayne's station wagon was well known around Newport Beach, and the manager must have called Wayne's house because before Lillian had the chance to confront her husband, Wayne himself was standing behind her.

"You must have really liked the car," Duke said, "because you never planned on giving it back to me."

Frank stood up. A young man appeared behind Wayne. Wayne nodded to Lillian and half nodded to the rest of the table. Jimmy smiled as though his dreams were all coming true, and Barbara held herself behind Jimmy as though she needed defense.

"We just stopped for a bite is all," Frank said. "And a little hair of the dog."

"Oh," Duke said, smiling at Lillian particularly, but smiling all around. "I know that dog. That's a *bad* dog."

Wayne approached the table and pulled up two chairs, forming an awkward semicircle around the circle of Frank's table. The young man who had driven him looked on. Jimmy and Barbara pulled over chairs from the other side of the room.

"That's okay, Bernard. You can go home now. Thanks for the ride."

Bernard, who seemed happy to be released from his responsibility, left the restaurant. As Lillian watched him go, she let herself imagine that John Wayne had come to make everything right. This wish was so concrete to her, and his help seemed so inevitable, that for a moment her body flushed with happiness.

"Have a seat, Lillian."

John Wayne drew a cigar from the vest pocket of his sport coat and accepted a matchbook that Jimmy tossed over the table. Jimmy's face was glowing. He'd met Duke before, but this was the first time Lillian had seen him so big with hope.

Watching Jimmy gave her the courage to watch Frank. Frank was sometimes more comfortable talking about John Wayne than actually being in his presence. His hands rambled the edge of the table, and his eyes were wide with bewildered cunning. To his credit, Frank wasn't a sycophant, but he was awed in a way that sometimes amounted to the same thing.

Wayne's motives were inscrutable. As he took his first self-pleasing puffs from the cigar, Lillian was trying to rationalize his immediate need for the car with his current laziness. As much as she would have enjoyed watching Frank squirm, she needed to make some sense of things.

"Don't you need to return the Christmas presents?"

Duke turned from his cigar and smiled at her.

"*They* want the Christmas presents," he said. "*I* want to smoke my goddamn cigar."

Phil smiled inexplicably. Frank raised his eyes toward Lillian. Jimmy and Barbara looked at each other. Danny watched his father.

"Everyone was so agitated," Wayne continued. "You would have thought I'd sold one of the kids into slavery. 'Where are the presents?' 'What's going to happen to the presents?' They wanted to know where you lived, whether it was a safe neighborhood, all sorts of crap. I didn't want to pester you, but it was choice between my pestering you and them pestering me. Now we're both free. Let's just relax and have some drinks and we'll all go home soon enough."

The waitress, as though listening for this sentence, appeared beside Lillian. "What would you like, Mr. Wayne?"

"I'd like an Irish coffee. Can you make me one of those?"

"Certainly."

"And whatever anyone else wants."

While Jimmy and Barbara and Phil made their drink orders, Lillian watched her husband sit before his nearly empty glass of scotch. In the company of John Wayne, she felt free of him, almost dispassionate. She didn't care whether Frank had another drink or not—she was going to divorce him anyway. As she settled into this new clarity, Duke touched her arm and asked for her order.

"I'll have a coffee."

Duke winked at the waitress. "Give her a little less whiskey than mine."

Lillian's voice rose in protest, but she found that she didn't have the heart to contradict him.

Danny turned his attention from his father to his mother. Lillian smiled and tried to project the thought that they would leave soon.

Duke, maybe realizing he was the only glue this party had, began to speak. Lillian imagined he was picking up some conversation from last night, but last night seemed further away than any other night of her life.

"The only good memory I have of Manhattan was getting drunk there with a bartender on the West Side. I just wandered off one night and I found this guy and we talked until the next morning. My heart was broken over some thing that I don't remember now, but I remember thinking, No one knows where I am, in the whole world, no one knows where I am but this goddamn bartender. Well, that was about as good as it ever got. Every other fucking time I was there, I hated it. It's such a nasty city. The whole deal there is about making everyone else feel stupid."

"What year was that?" Lillian asked.

"With the bartender? That must have been '57 or '58."

Lillian leaned back. The drinks arrived. Frank had ordered another scotch, and she was happy not to care anymore. Her own Irish coffee looked too hot to touch.

"Frank and I were broken up for a while," Lillian said. "That was about the time I went to Bermuda with a bunch of my girlfriends."

"I wish I could remember the name of the bar," Wayne said. "Sometimes I think I'd like to give that guy a call or send him a picture or something. If he's still alive."

"What neighborhood was it in?" Frank asked, clearing his throat.

"Hell, I don't know neighborhoods in New York. It was near Broadway on the West Side."

"Hell's Kitchen?" Jimmy offered hopefully. "Maybe it was Hell's Kitchen?"

"I don't know," Wayne said. "That could be right." Duke took a sip of his Irish coffee, which seemed to give everyone else permission to take sips from their own drinks. Frank picked up his scotch and then put it down again. He seemed sad and uncertain. His son watched him and seemed to sadden, too, although Danny did take a sip from his Shirley Temple after freeing the cherry from its stem and carefully eating it.

"Hell's Kitchen," Phil said absently. "What a scary name."

"Irish, it's all Irish," Jimmy added. He looked to Barbara, Lillian thought, rather than to Wayne. "It's all Irish there."

For a while, everyone just drank their drinks and watched John Wayne. Danny finished first, and as though this gave him some new freedom, he smiled around the table at everyone, forcing everyone to smile back at him. Everyone could feel that the party was over, but Danny and John Wayne were the first to recognize it. Wayne stood up from the table, pushing himself off Lillian's chair and then holding her by the shoulder. She turned to watch his hand. It was puffy with age, but still gracefully formed. He was holding her, but he was also leaning on her.

"And now I really ought to return those goddamn Christmas presents."

Among the rest of the party, only Frank stood with him. "All right," Frank announced. "Thanks for having a drink with us, Duke."

"Well, thanks for bringing my car back, Frank." Lillian thought she heard mockery in Duke's tone. Her husband and Wayne faced each other awkwardly, neither of them quite able to get to the next thing in their lives until Lillian realized what the problem was.

"The keys, Frank."

Quickly, Frank brought up the keys and handed them to Duke. Duke touched his forehead and nodded to the table before he walked out of the restaurant.

Lillian could feel the vacuum left by Duke's departure, and it made her sad to be so suddenly back in ordinary reality. Everyone at the table seemed empty. Unspectacular drunkenness and drug addiction were showing in Frank's and Jimmy's eyes. Barbara and

Phil were completely bewildered by their part in this drama. Danny stared at his mother.

"It's time to go home," Lillian said.

The waitress appeared beside her. "Mr. Wayne has taken care of it. You don't owe me anything." She spoke with small enthusiasm, as though she'd absorbed the malaise of the table.

Everyone started to leave but Frank, who seemed to be taking inventory of the scotch left in his glass. Lillian realized that he hadn't yet touched it, but the story wasn't over. As long as Duke sat with them, Frank's life had coherence. But now Frank was about to leave the restaurant for a life he could do nothing to prevent.

Danny, maybe knowing all that Lillian knew, offered him the courage to get home. "Come on, Dad, let's go." Lillian couldn't guess whether it was generosity or irritation on Danny's part, but it seemed to do the trick. Frank walked away from the last drink of the morning.

As they left the restaurant together, Frank seemed bolder as a result of his self-denial. He walked beside his wife, and when she opened her car door, he stood right behind her and placed his hand on the roof.

"What are you doing?" Lillian asked.

"I think we should drive home together," Frank said.

"Leave me alone."

Danny appeared at the passenger door, testing the handle, but not opening.

"We need to talk," Frank said.

"Don't fucking touch me." Leaving the car and Danny behind her, Lillian faced her husband. For the first time that day, she let him look at her. She didn't back away. She didn't slouch. She couldn't hide from herself anymore the thought that had been behind everything all day long—she wished he were dead. Everything would be so much simpler if Frank were just dead.

She almost smiled at the simplicity of the thought that came to her next: she couldn't afford to feel that way about her husband. A woman who could feel that way about her husband was the wrong kind of woman—a tremendously unfortunate human being. She wouldn't stand for it a minute longer.

"Get a lawyer, Frank. I don't ever want to talk to you again."

Danny opened the passenger door, and he sat down in the seat meant for his father. Frank bent down and watched him through the window. Danny looked back with a kind of sullen victory. He was tired, Lillian could see, and he couldn't bear to help his father anymore.

Frank walked away, and Lillian started her car without watching him leave. As she turned onto Pacific Coast Highway and drove past the marine supply stores and restaurants and bars and beach clubs, she imagined herself a powerful woman who had just finished taking control of her life.

"Are you really going to get divorced?" Danny asked.

As she looked over at him, she remarked to herself for the thousandth time what a strange child he was. He watched her now with as much intensity as he had watched his father earlier.

"Yes," she said. "You don't think it's a good idea?"

"You have to."

"Thanks for understanding that, sweetheart. Your father's going to be okay. We're all going to be okay."

Danny had a large sharp head and dark serious eyes. He watched his parents as though his life depended on the outcome of their marriage. She was certain that her inability and fear had hurt him—maybe even before he was born—but she couldn't think about that today. She had too much to do. She made a mental shopping list of what would be required of her over the next few weeks—a meeting with a lawyer, a talk with her children, a restraining order—but none of it seemed so insurmountable as it had a few hours earlier.

"Are you going to start working again?" Danny asked.

"As long as you've been alive, I've never worked for anyone but your father, but I've always worked."

"You *know* what I mean. You're going to be finished with school soon. I was just wondering."

"I was thinking about teaching."

"That's a good idea, but don't teach at my school."

"No, I don't think I want to teach at your school, honey."

She turned left at the intersection of Coast Highway and Jamboree. The haze was starting to burn off the beach towns, and she was no longer afraid of the coast, now that she was leaving it. The hills near Fashion Island were richly green, like the hills of some other country.

They just drove for a while without talking. Danny seemed more comfortable than he'd been all morning. He'd resisted her since the day he was born, but sometimes he resisted her less. She wondered what he'd be like if he'd had a different father. She tried to imagine him as Michael's son, and then John Wayne's, and then Phil's. She imagined him as a Jew, the son of a movie star, a quiet boy growing up in Lompoc. Each time, she had to deprive Danny of his essential quality, the quality she didn't think he could live without—his vast sadness.

"What do you think of John Wayne?" Lillian asked.

"Not too much."

"You're not impressed with such a big movie star?"

"He's an old man. He drinks as much as Dad does."

115

"How do you know that?"

"I can just tell."

When she reached the end of Milford Road, her driveway and curb were thick with cars. She wanted to reach out her hand and swat them all away. She had imagined she was returning to her own home, but this thickness of vehicles proved that Frank still considered it his home, too. As she parked across the street in front of Mary Beth's house and counted them—her husband's pickup, her husband's Buick, Jimmy's antique Cadillac, Phil and Arlene's absurd camper—she realized that she couldn't go inside. She couldn't stomach another moment of any of them. Danny was once again staring at her, his face disorganized by anxiety.

"I'm going to take a little drive," Lillian said. "You go into the house and tell everybody I'll be back later." As she said it, she didn't know if it was true.

"We just *took* a little drive," Danny said. "I want to come with you."

"Listen, nothing bad's going to happen except everything bad that's already happened. You've been a great friend to me today, but now I need to be alone." She wondered how honest she could afford to be. "I just can't stand the thought of talking with any of them right now. Do you understand that?"

"I don't want to talk with any of them, either."

"But, sweetheart, you'll be the only sane man I'll know in that house, and I'm going to need a sane man in that house."

"I'm not a man. I'm a boy."

"Don't be smartass. You know what I mean."

And it seemed he did know what she meant. But what she meant was nothing like what she was saying. What she meant was: I need everyone in one place so that I can get away from you all.

She smiled with great care and kissed him on the cheek. He slowly removed himself from the car and walked across the street while she watched him.

She turned left on Tustin Avenue and tried to avoid the whole issue of the freeway. After a few miles of pushing through the small businesses and shopping centers that clotted along the road, she realized she was driving in a familiar direction, toward Tustin, where Frank's office and shop were. The truth was she had nowhere else to go and Frank would never think to look for her there.

It was as she drove toward the lumberyard where Frank rented a building that she first imagined she might never see her children again. She dismissed the thought, but the flavor of her thinking had been changed. In her thoughts, she was moving toward the kind of hell her mother had promised her, a place for people who embraced their desires rather than their duties.

And so, by the time she sat down at the first desk in the front room of the office—*her* desk—she was compulsively thinking about Michael Grau. As the dusty chair squeaked beneath her, she had to admit that her memories of him were hard to grasp. The two years before she met Frank were years of hope and desolation. They were the years in which she'd gone to college and then decided to quit college. They were also the years when it became clear that she would have to marry a Catholic or give up any hope of her mother's love. Consequently, what she remembered was garbled by self-justification and hatred. Some things she couldn't remember at all. What was it like when she started Hunter College? She didn't know. What was it like when she decided to quit Hunter College? She didn't know that, either. She'd noticed this effect before. At certain milestones in her children's development, for example, she had tried to remember herself at that age and discovered that where once there might have been a memory, now there was only imagination.

But Michael was her lost life come alive. She danced her fingers across the adding machine and sat up straight in the old office chair. His face was at the center of a vacuum that was the most important years of her life. His face was at the center of a decision she hadn't yet made.

What did she remember? He talked a lot about the cars he would one day have, she remembered that. He seemed to know everything there was to know about the French Foreign Legion. He always stood up from the table when Lillian introduced one of her girlfriends, and he dressed much better than his income. She also remembered that when he kissed her, she couldn't tell where his mouth ended and hers began. Kissing him was like finding her home, unexpectedly, just around a corner, in a city she'd never been to before.

She arrived at her desire just as a compressor on the far end of the building erupted into rhythm. Her fingers abandoned the adding machine and touched the telephone.

She got his number from the operator. He picked up on the third ring and spoke his last name clearly.

"It's Lillian Barden."

He waited for a moment before responding. "I liked Hedendal better. Not that Barden's a bad name, it just doesn't sound right."

"I never liked Hedendal," Lillian admitted. "It never sounded like a real person's name."

Lillian considered the decoration in her husband's office. There were framed drawings of houses he'd built, one of them the house he'd built for her. There was a framed photograph of John Wayne on the wall beside the file cabinets. A light dust covered everything, a gift from the cabinet shop next door.

"What was I like when I was Lillian Hedendal?" she asked. She tried to give her tone a lightness that she didn't feel.

"You were a tall, skinny girl with the energy of five tall, skinny girls."

Lillian's stomach shrank. She could feel the way he'd kissed her and it was like remembering a time when she'd lived in someone else's body. She looked around the office for some detail that might bring her back. Beneath the air conditioner on a small wooden table stood the ceramic priest they'd bought in Tijuana the year Chris was born. Everything was quiet except for the humming of the compressor in the background.

"You still don't remember me?" Michael asked.

"Not very well."

Lillian wanted to hang up the phone, but it seemed too late for that. If she hung up now, she'd only call back later, and that would be one more humiliation in a day full of humiliations.

"Then I'm wondering why you called me?"

"I don't know," Lillian said. "I remember dating somebody like you."

She was beginning to feel dusty sitting in this chair. She could feel the dust settling into her skin.

"Who do you think I am, then?" Michael asked.

She stared at the door to the cabinet shop, the source of all that dust.

"I know who I am," Michael said. "I'm the ghost of every bad decision you've ever made."

"You're a smart boy, aren't you?"

All of Frank's tools were waiting there in the darkness of the cabinet shop. The compressor was only one thing that might waken into frightening life. There were jigsaws and sanders and routers and planers and so many other things to fear.

She leaned back and closed her eyes. The chair squealed like something dying. She could see Michael's face. He was handsome, but empty of the kind of sacrifice Lillian had made. Children, even when you were abandoning them, left marks all over you. Michael's face was radiant with good health. He had always slept enough. He had always been admired by his friends. His eyes were dark, but unconscious of real darkness.

She started to speak, but then she didn't speak. Again, Michael spoke for her.

"It sounds like you're having a rough time."

Lillian laughed. The compressor stopped pumping, and the silence that resulted was louder than the noise.

"I'm not looking for anything in particular here," Michael continued. "But I think you're better than any of the trouble he's been giving you. Maybe it's time to get out."

"I have kids."

"That's just an excuse."

"Did you want to marry me?" Lillian asked. "I mean, before."

"I might have."

"Why didn't I let you?"

"Because I was Jewish, probably. What do you think?"

"Yeah, that's probably it."

"I apologize, but from my perspective, it feels like no time has passed at all. Last night, you looked like the same girl I dated from Hunter College."

"Thanks, I think."

"Oh, it's a compliment, Lillian. Don't worry about it. It's a compliment."

"You're mad?"

"Hey, I don't look for this kind of trouble in my life, but when it comes, I'd rather deal with it. Just tell me why you called me. That should help."

Suddenly, she remembered it all. In her mind's eye, she saw a moment fifteen years earlier when a boy—and that boy was Michael—had pleaded with her to change her mind. Michael wasn't pleading with her now, but his *request* came from the same distant source—a nervous desire that she do the right thing. Then, as now, she was appalled by how much power he thought she had. Then, as now, the idea that she could reject him made her feel strong and free and terrified.

As she stood from the chair, a part of her was three thousand miles and fifteen years away from this shitty little side building at the end of the Mullen Lumber parking lot. She was watching Michael's face near an ice skating rink in Manhattan, and she was deciding why she didn't want to see him anymore.

She had felt compelled to throw him away because she didn't know how she would live if she kept him. She didn't know how she could become the wife of a Jew any more than she knew how she could become the wife of a man who spoke so earnestly with her about all that she was interested in. Michael had taken her to jazz clubs and foreign films and restaurants without liquor licenses. He listened carefully to what she said, and he *knew why* that was important. He was beautiful, and kissing him made her wet between the legs. There was nothing she could do but turn him away. It must have been shortly after that when she quit college.

Standing in the middle of Barden Construction Company,

feeling the thick dust settle into her skin, she was aware of herself as the same woman who had thrown away Michael, who had quit college, who had been enthusiastic to do both.

"You don't know what you want to do next," Michael said. "I can tell."

"You're a mind reader now?"

"No, I'm just a man who wants your attention and can tell when he's not getting it."

It was thrilling to remember. She'd had a childhood of screaming mothers, and poor baskets, and no room for herself, and no father, and maybe Michael had been present for the only moment in her younger life when she could have turned her direction.

"I have to go now," Lillian said.

Lillian could imagine the arguments he might make. She could make them herself. But Michael didn't say anything.

"I'm going now," Lillian said.

"This is almost as abrupt as it was the last time," Michael said.

"There wasn't any last time," Lillian said. "You dreamed that up."

It was late afternoon. The sky was immense and startling. The trees, which had been planted only a few years before, poked up at it.

Her driveway was empty. Frank's truck was parked on the street, and she guessed that the Buick must be in the garage. Jimmy's Cadillac was parked thoughtfully in front of Mary Beth's house. Lillian paused beside Phil and Arlene's camper, feeling protected for one last moment before she turned into her driveway.

The day had become warm and she imagined them all on the patio, admiring Frank's latest project.

She turned in front of the barrier that separated Milford Road from the new development, and she parked on the left side of the driveway, knowing that the Buick would be on the right side of the garage. She had never disliked her own house so much. The concrete, which she had watched Frank pour; the grass, which she had chosen herself; even the high-quality shake shingles on the roof—all of it seemed obscene. As she turned off the ignition and set the parking brake, she tried to imagine herself a much braver woman than she had shown herself to be.

Frank was already at the door when she walked around the garage toward the house. Because he was sober, he was bruised and incapacitated. She had spent six months of her twenty-second year studying his face and wondering if he could be trusted to provide a life for her. Now she saw what she might have seen then: the eyes of a child, not a man who would learn anything from his pain, but a child who was bound to be overwhelmed by it. What had happened to him that he could afford to be so terrified of his life?

As she approached the door, Frank backed away from it.

"Chris is asleep, and the kids are playing in the backyard," he said.

"Where's Arlene and Phil?"

"They're out on the patio with my brother and . . ."

"Barbara."

She walked past him into the living room, where the curtains were drawn and the Christmas tree glowed with annoying cheerfulness in the far corner. Her daughter insisted that it be left on all the time during the holiday season. Lillian sat down on the couch near the fireplace. For a moment uncertain, Frank chose the recliner on the other side of the room. Once sitting, he looked as though he regretted the choice. Lillian could feel his tremendous awkwardness, like a pain in his groin, and she wished she had more of this pain to give.

"Where'd you go?" Frank asked.

"None of your goddamn business."

In the dim light, she saw a cardboard box beside the fireplace, looking like a dreary unwrapped Christmas present. She wanted to ask Frank what it was, but she didn't want to hear his answer, so she stood up from the couch and walked to the fireplace. In block letters not at all like her own, the box was labeled JOHN WAYNE MEM.

"What the hell does 'MEM' mean?" she asked.

"Memorabilia," Frank said. "I wasn't sure how to spell it, and you weren't around to ask."

"Is that what you did while I was gone?"

"Arlene fixed lunch, and then she put Chris down to sleep. I was showing some stuff to Phil and Jimmy, and afterwards I thought I should give it all one home. I took one of the packing boxes from the garage."

Frank had collected everything he could find of John Wayne in the house, and then put it all into this box beside the fireplace. He was more of a child than she knew. She pulled on the top flap of the box and turned it over onto the living room floor. Mostly paper and trinkets, the contents spilled like liquid onto the carpet, spreading nearly three feet into the room. She watched Frank as his body stiffened. She wished he had the courage to beat her for what she was about to do to him.

What covered the floor was unknowable at first. The living room was too murky to see much. Lillian bent over and grabbed a handful to bring back to the couch with her. Sitting down, she switched on the lamp beside her. The new light startled Frank's face into clarity.

The first was a picture of John Wayne with his youngest son, Ethan, who was about Alice's age. Duke was wearing the eyepatch from *True Grit*. His son wore one, too. Wayne was looking toward the sky and seemed to forget about his son beside him. His son was also looking toward the sky. Lillian thought it was a picture about distance and loss and the inability to love well. At the moment the photo was taken, Duke must have been very tired.

Lillian shuffled the picture back into the pile. Behind it was a Polaroid of her son Danny standing in the backyard holding a rifle that was a foot taller than he was. She held that picture up. Frank leaned forward.

"It's a Revolutionary War rifle we brought home one afternoon to show Danny. I don't know where you were that day."

She tossed the rest of the pictures aside, but set the Polaroid of Danny on the end table beside the couch. She returned to the pile of papers on the floor and spread them even farther into the room. From underneath another *True Grit* publicity shot, she extracted a Zippo lighter bearing the inscription SPECIAL FORCES. DA NANG. IT'S A GOOD DAY TO DIE. She threw it at Frank, who awkwardly caught it between his forearm and chest. He inspected it.

"It's from *The Green Berets*," he said. "Someone must have given it to Duke when he was over there filming. Duke gave it to me."

"You don't smoke."

"I know."

Lillian abandoned the contents of the JOHN WAYNE MEM box and returned to the couch, where she looked one more time at the photo of her son. The picture had been taken sideways so that the length of the gun would be even more dramatic.

"You want to go outside, on the patio?" Frank asked.

She was so tired of him. As she began to cry, the Christmas

tree sparkled and the whole room softened. She could hear her own breath as though it were being squeezed from her body.

"I can't do this anymore," Lillian said. She cleared her eyes with the back of her hand and stared past the Christmas tree into the dining room, where her youngest son was standing inexpertly, mesmerized by the light.

"Oh, sweetheart!" Lillian hurried toward him. "How did you get so far into the house by yourself?"

Christopher smiled, stunned by the sudden attention but eager to shift his focus from the tree to his mother. He lifted his arms as though he would condescend to fly toward her, and she picked him up as though he were the sweetest package she would ever lift. Christopher squealed and shouted and tried to make sentences from his unexpected happiness as Lillian carried him back to the couch. Surveying the festive room over his mother's shoulder, he locked gazes with his father, who was cajoled into a smile.

"He's the happiest child," Lillian said to someone, but probably not to Frank. "Of the three of them, he's the happiest. He loves Christmas even more than Alice. Don't you, sweetheart?"

Frank stared at the back of his son's head. He knew when to keep his mouth shut.

"He really pulls the other two together," Lillian continued. "The only time they work with each other anymore is when they're trying to make him laugh."

She lifted Christopher and swung him from his shoulders. He held his breath for a moment before he was certain she would not throw him across the room, and then he smiled in a way that would have been horrible for anyone but a child. Frank sat forward in his chair.

Alice and Danny appeared beside each other where the living room met the hallway. Alice was holding a book in her right hand, but Danny's hands were empty. Lillian smiled at them and set Chris down beside her.

"Look at my two sweethearts," Lillian said. "Why aren't you over here with your mother?"

The children stepped down into the sunken living room and cautiously approached her. Lillian felt very old, but still miraculously adequate to their grief.

"Did you have a good day?" Lillian asked.

Alice smiled as though she knew what the question really meant, and Danny just stared.

Alice said, "Arlene helped me draw pictures of the people in the neighborhood, and then she said that her pictures weren't as good as mine."

"Will you show me later?"

"Okay."

"And what did you do this afternoon, Danny?"

Danny looked past her and his face tightened. He was starting to look like his father, but he was still soft and skinny, like Lillian herself. She could tell that she had betrayed him, but she wasn't sure which way her betrayal cut. Was he angry because she had left or angry because she had returned?

"I helped Dad in the garage. We got some of that John Wayne stuff together."

"Can we open some Christmas presents tonight?" Alice asked. "While Arlene and Phil are still here."

The wrapped boxes in front of the tree were just tokens, but Alice didn't know that. Lillian would wrap the *real* presents much closer to Christmas. She took a lot of care with Christmas—

although Frank often spoiled it—because it was her job, as deeply and importantly as anything had ever been her job. Was it her job to let Frank fuck her? No. Was it her job to be humiliated in front of famous men and women? No. But it was her job to design and execute a Christmas that not one of her children would be dissatisfied with.

Two hours earlier, she'd had a moment when she could have walked away from all of it. But now that moment had passed. What had happened here while she was gone? What was the important thing she had missed? Why was she here again, in the middle of a marriage she hated and children she couldn't possibly love well enough?

Frank watched her carefully. He knew she was somewhere else, but he was afraid to ask where. The children were disturbed by her sudden silence and they kept silent themselves.

After she had hung up on Michael, she stood for a long time staring at the walls of Frank's office. They were paneled with dark wood veneer, and they made her feel safe from a world of other people. She thought about everything that had happened that day, which became everything that had happened in the last ten years. The dark walls told stories about leaving New York, about long, painful births, about working late into the night as a small construction company began to grow. From the doorway of her husband's office, she watched First Street and wondered if she would ever have the courage to drive away.

That was probably the moment, she realized now, when the box came out and John Wayne was assembled in her living room. As she sat between her husband and her children, Lillian's imagination of that moment took on the clarity of a vision, like the first time she saw Manhattan, like Bernadette seeing the Blessed Virgin, like seeing her babies' eyes opened up after her own huge pain. As clearly as she could see the Christmas tree sparkling across the room, she could see Danny emerging from the hallway with some treasure of Frank's recent employment. No distance or device would have let her escape this scene. There were many things, she knew, that hadn't been put into the box, larger or more dangerous objects that lived in careful corners of her house. In her vision, Frank was distributing posters and framed pictures and Green Beret cigarette lighters and commemorative handguns and big knives and even a box of cigars. The joy that these trivial objects brought to Lillian's house was unexpected and almost miraculous, and she could see that it wasn't the simple joy of small people who longed for a bigger, brighter world, but the complicated joy of broken-hearted people who desperately needed something between them, something more substantial than sandwiches and soda pop.

Frank was getting more concerned. He leaned forward in the recliner and threatened to stand. He wouldn't abide her silence a moment longer. His arms tightened as the chair creaked and stuttered. His children stared at him, hoping that somehow he would help her.

Lillian cried as her imagination touched both Frank's weakness and his strength. She cried because she knew he wanted to be a great man, had sacrificed a lot for his dreams, had worked hard to be as sturdy as he was. She cried, too, because he was such a piece of shit as a husband and a father. For all the moments like this one, when she could see his beauty and his strength, there were moments just afterward when she knew that he was incapable of satisfying anyone around him.

She knew what presents were in the back of John Wayne's station wagon. They weren't the irreplaceable treasures that she had imagined—they were the ordinary gifts that only Lillian Barden couldn't afford. A good marriage was in one box, the good men she might have married in another. Happy vacations and pleasant Sunday afternoons and parties where wives could be proud of their husbands—all those gifts were there, too, wrapped boldly and scattered around the back of the station wagon like an afterthought. None of it would ever belong to her, though. Her husband was a drunk, and he would continue to steal from her life with his false bravery and ineffective strength. John Wayne himself was an illusion, and Frank Barden was even further from the truth than that. The world was small. And no one in it had much power over themselves.

Men Without Women

1975

It had started—he could pinpoint the day, the hour—two months earlier when his daughter Aissa, in an idle conversation while she followed him through his early morning walk, suggested he might be old enough and tractable enough finally to learn Spanish. All of his wives, Aissa reminded him, and most of his children spoke it with native fluency. He'd come to expect this kind of suggestion from Aissa, who was entering a bright period of her adolescence. She had a boyfriend, she was getting ready to go away to school, and she was full of schemes to improve her father. Most of his children had gone through the same phase, but he'd never been so present for it as he was with Aissa.

As she went on, warming to her father-improvement program, she suggested that he take lessons from Ernesto—their butler—whom her father loved very much. And it was this notion which transformed Aissa's meddling into something deeper and more enduring. Duke could *see* that, he could see spending afternoons with Ernesto at the round table, just indoors but maybe a breeze gathering behind the curtains to make their conversation—*¡en español!*—blossom with the significance of a lifetime spent putting off this important task. Yes, he could *see* that.

He held Aissa by the neck and kissed her on the temple, the way he'd loved to do since she was a downy-haired child. He said, "That's a good idea, sweetheart. I'm gonna do that."

From that day, the power of his resolve grew. Every afternoon for several weeks he spent with Ernesto, his Mexican friend drilling him with simple words for the simple objects that surrounded him. Duke's world began to change because he was seeing it through the eyes of a language that was at once completely familiar and totally strange. His house was no longer his home, it was *su hogar*. His boat was no longer his last refuge, it was *su barco*. His children, three of whom were still in the house, were nothing more than *hijos* to him. Even the flagpole, which sat at the end of the lawn above Newport Bay, had been changed completely. It was *asta de una bandera*.

Somehow, within the refraction that learning Spanish created for him, Duke began to think about his life in ways that would

have scared anyone but Ernesto, who Duke now felt could understand anything. There were parts of himself he hadn't explored
since he was a teenager, since before he entered the movie business, and many of these lost pieces of his personality were calling
for his attention like meddling teenagers themselves.

What were these teenagers saying to him? *Silly* things—so
silly that at first they seemed beyond Duke's ability to comprehend. They said, for example, that the country he was born in, the
country he had spent a lifetime celebrating, could no longer be his
home, that this country had disappointed him too profoundly, that
he could no longer dignify it with his presence. This was the
teenager of high ideals and patriotism. The teenager of restlessness
and glee suggested that he move to Mexico, where he could spend
the rest of his life speaking Spanish, eating good fresh food, breathing good fresh air, and watching the waves roll in toward some
mostly glass, sunlight-flooded beach house. Within five weeks after
Aissa's suggestion, it had become clear to him that he must leave
the United States. It was the only thing left for him to do.

And therefore, one day in late October, he found himself in
his station wagon, pounding up the hill toward Corona del Mar,
past Chick Iverson's Porsche/Audi dealership, past the mouth of
Newport Bay, and past Hemingway's, a *restorán* that he liked very
much. He was pretty certain he wasn't leaving town just yet, but,
then again, he had no destination except *south*. As he drove past
MacArthur Boulevard, which might take him to the *aeropuerto,* he
was forced to slow down through the abundant traffic lights of
Corona del Mar, and he felt himself at peace in a way he hadn't
experienced since he was a kid. The sky above the coast was pink
and gray, and he didn't feel any anxiety to speed up the traffic. For
a few blocks he stayed behind a dithering Volkswagen just to see
what it felt like to move that slowly on purpose.

He remembered the last time he felt this kind of conviction. It was at the start of his professional life, the day he volunteered to be John Ford's stuntman on the submarine adventure *Men Without Women*. He was still a propman then, trying to steady himself on a boat a few miles off Catalina in seas so heavy that even the stuntmen balked. Duke stepped forward, dove into the high waves, and doubled for four different actors who were supposed to escape from a drowning submarine. In retrospect, it was the best thing he could have done for his career. The joke of it was that he had thought no more than a man running from a burning house: his instinct to help Ford was too deep to be articulated.

He would just keep driving south for a while, past Dana Point, past San Clemente, past La Jolla and the Scripps Clinic, maybe even as far as the Mexican border. He thought of it as a trial run for the day when he would take this trip for the last time.

There weren't many unrehearsed moments in his life: he could count maybe three times when he had proceeded without calculating the consequences. In these cases, it had been because some image of Ford was brooding above him and he was called forward by the need to please that brilliant old drunk.

As he passed Crystal Cove, a pleasant little nick in the coastline, he remembered the day Ford died. All that day, he felt brutalized by his grief. It had been years since he'd given Pappy the respect he deserved. Oh, he made a show of it—appearing at awards ceremonies and making all the proper noises for the press. But they both knew he was just too old and too famous and too rich to jump into the water like that anymore. The last time Duke saw the old man out in Palm Desert, the meeting stunk like the arrival of a visiting dignitary or a distant relative or an ungrateful son.

As he floated over the ridge into Laguna Beach proper, past

Irvine Cove, past Emerald Bay, the Pacific Ocean rising and then falling behind him like a blanket shook over a bed, he remembered how he and Ward used to make this same drive during World War II, drunk out of their minds, running from some imagined enemy toward some imagined friend. In those days, they were always a little somber with the understanding that Ford was on the other side of the world, risking his life to film some battle. To each other, they were conspicuously absent from the war. They were making more money than they'd ever made before, and Duke kept thinking, Just one more picture, just one more picture, and then I'll enlist. Once, driving down this same road, Ward couldn't stop talking about how he'd use a high-powered rifle to eliminate all the queers from Laguna Beach, which was, even then, a very queer town. For reasons he couldn't account for, Duke suddenly regretted this talk and wished he could reach back in time and stop Ward from making that memory between them. This afternoon, he wouldn't be able to tell the queers from anyone else. He wished he'd treated Rock Hudson better. He wished he'd given Jerry Brown his vote. Someday, they would all be *camaradas*.

Right now, though, he had to get something to eat.

He parked just off Pacific Coast Highway, beside a restaurant he liked very much called The Cottage. It was a simple place, a converted home. The light in the dining room reminded him of calm dusky afternoons in his mother's house, when he would dream of commanding a battleship, the dust motes gathering in the sunshine like sparkling bits of desire. He told the young blond waiter with the pageboy haircut that there was only one of him, that he wanted a table in the dusty sunlight if he could arrange it. People in Orange County always knew that John Wayne might show up and they tried to act unsurprised. The waiter's "Yes, sir" seemed a little forced, as though all the tension of his restraint had been pushed into it. He grabbed a stack of menus. It was late afternoon and the restaurant was close to empty, but heads turned anyway.

"Is this okay, Mr. Wayne?" The young man's face went dark for a second as he reckoned whether it was permissible to know John Wayne's name.

"This is great. Just the way I wanted it. Do you have a newspaper I could read while I eat?"

"No, but I could get you one down the street."

"That would be great. Thanks."

Although he was powerfully built and athletic, this young man was also pretty like a girl. Duke decided not to be bothered by it. There was a time almost fifty years ago when he himself was pretty like a girl.

He ordered a club sandwich with lots of mayo and a side of fries. When the young man returned with the newspapers—he'd brought the *Los Angeles Times* and the *Orange County Register*—his face was screwed up into some sort of decision. He wasn't as afraid of Duke as before, but he wasn't particularly calm, either.

"Mr. Wayne, can I ask you a question?"

He stared up at the boy, and as his meal arrived, he resisted the temptation to take a fry. He gave him his full attention.

"Do you think a girl—almost a woman really—should be able to date anyone she wants to? I mean, do you think that parents should be able to tell a teenager who she can and cannot date?"

It was a bizarre question that spoke for the intensity of the whole afternoon. Was Duke talking to the girl right now? Was this boy *un maricón?* He'd never wanted to know that much about queers, but this was a day when it would have come in handy.

"What are we talking about here?"

"Sir?"

"This is a girl you're going out with?"

"This is a girl I *was* going out with until her parents told her she couldn't."

Duke was relieved, but still confused. "Now, why didn't they like you?"

"I think they don't like the haircut and they don't like surfers."

"You're a surfer?"

"Yes, sir."

"And you want me to tell you what to do?"

"That would be nice, sir."

Duke tried to imagine this boy with fifty more years on his head, at the end of a long career, having made and lost a few fortunes, having had his heart broken by each fortune and the woman that went with it. He was handsome enough to be a lead— he was just the kind of boy the studios used to scoop up from beaches and football teams. Just the kind of boy that Duke himself used to be.

"You're not an actor, are you?" Duke asked.

"No."

"Ever thought about it?"

"No, sir."

"Don't even think about it. It's a stupid fucking profession. Listen, just date her behind their backs. She'll do that, won't she? Big, good-looking guy like you. Hell, I stole my last wife from right off her first husband's lap."

"Mr. Wayne, are you making fun of me?"

"No, of course not." He smiled and reached for his sandwich.

"You really think that's what I should do?"

"Yes, that's what I think you should do. What? You want me to talk to her parents for you? They're not going to listen to me."

The boy meant well. By his girlfriend, by her parents, by John Wayne. But the truth was he didn't know shit. His worries were irrelevant. Life filtered down into more and more essential questions: "Would you like more coffee, Mr. Wayne? Can I get you anything else?" Eating and driving and going to Mexico were all he wanted to think about today. Today, he wanted to be a man with nothing on his mind but satisfying his most basic needs. All summer, Richard Nixon would crank up the air conditioning at the White House so that he could have a big roaring fire. Today, John Wayne wanted to be that kind of man.

The passage from Laguna was anticlimactic. Sometimes, when he tired of the conspicuous consumption of Newport, he imagined that Laguna would have been a better place to settle. But his dreams of the town were always much better than the town itself. He wanted it to be more quaint and homey than it was. Driving up the hill toward Aliso Beach, he fell into a revery about all that he might have done if he hadn't made the most obvious choices. He imagined himself on the deck of a cruiser, forty years out of Annapolis, near the end of a glorious career. Three wars? Yes, he would have fought in three wars. And then he imagined himself a lawyer who had triumphed over nepotism and corruption with hard work and ingenuity. A partnership? A bench? Would he have gone into politics? He didn't begrudge himself the choices he'd made, and he wasn't feeling sorry for himself. It was pleasant to think this way.

As he passed Dana Point toward San Clemente, he had to

think about Nixon again. There was no way to avoid Nixon these days. His shadow had darkened everything in the county for three years. San Clemente itself was such a sparkling old-world town— filled with bougainvillea and palm trees—but it could get so dark sometimes with Nixon's defeat. Duke's problem, like everyone else's, was that he held Dick too close. Duke had taken it personally when he resigned. It had felt like the cowardice of everyone Duke knew.

The landscape beyond San Clemente was a relief from an advancing Orange County. As long as there was need to defend the United States, this land would be owned by the Marine Corps and they would keep it as wild and undeveloped as they liked. As the highway thinned and the traffic disappeared, he pleased himself by imagining that this was the kind of earth his parents had brought him across on their way to California. He looked to his left and he could see the brown hills gathering toward the gray sky. When he looked to his right, he saw the Pacific Ocean beating toward the edge of North America. For a moment, he was gloomy with all he was going to leave behind.

But that wasn't going to stop him. By now, the waiter had told the cook and the waitress what a weird old bird John Wayne was. By now, his family was wondering where he'd gone. By now, the first inscrutable reports of his defection were reaching ears that could not hear to hear, as his absence was wasted on eyes that could not see to see. They were, all of them, *menso*. Hoping to put more distance between himself and all the people who thought they understood him, he stomped his foot farther toward the floor and pushed the car ahead of himself another ten miles per hour.

What the waiter didn't know was that no one was watching. No one gave a shit what he did or whom he did it with, even the people closest to him, even the people who pretended to care.

Duke could empathize because he'd spent most of his life believing that they were watching him, but now that he was old and comfortable and full of all the bullshit that one nation could pour into a man, he no longer kidded himself that there was any judgment beyond his own. And if this brown and scratchy landscape—this *chaparral*—didn't judge itself, neither would he. What that waiter didn't understand was that his girlfriend's parents would hate him no matter what he did.

About a mile ahead of him, he could see a line of stopped vehicles. For the last few minutes, Duke had imagined the highway as his own. He squinted through the windshield and let off the gas. It was an accident or a checkpoint or something, and he hated it the way he had once hated communism, and for the same reason—because it threatened to legislate his desire. In a few minutes, he was behind a row of cars and trucks that stood dumbfounded on the asphalt. He strained and stuck his head out the window. As far as he could see around the bend, nothing moved.

He got out of his station wagon. As he walked along the line of cars, he remembered the last thing the waiter had said to him. "I thought you'd be more helpful than that. I'm sorry I bothered you."

Well, that was it, wasn't it? That's what he imagined the whole goddamn country saying to him now that he was leaving. They all sounded like such whiners lately. Even the men he had once admired like Goldwater and Nixon. Whiners. Reagan and Buckley. Whiners. Heston and Stewart. Whiners all of them. *Chillones*.

The embankment was baked hard as concrete. As he made his way forward, some of the people who had stayed in their cars watched him, but mostly they didn't. They were stuck to their lives as certainly as their cars were stuck to the road. Large men like himself walked forward, but they didn't notice him, either. The mystery of their inactivity seemed to be consuming everyone's attention.

He decided not to look anyone in the eye and continued forward. The curving bushy embankment retreated from him until he reached the start of the long line of cars. In the middle of the two-lane road, there was a T formed where a Ford pickup had been centerpunched by an old Impala. The arrangement of these cars was so strange and perfect that it looked as though it had been staged.

He stood off a little, trying not to attract attention. A group of men looked on as a young man and an older man shouted at each other beside the T of cars. From the position of their bodies, Duke guessed that the young man owned the pickup and the older man owned the Impala. At that moment, the onlookers seemed to be rallying themselves toward a decision. No one was hurt, and they would begin to drive their cars around the accident. Duke would have returned to his station wagon just then had he not seen something beyond the accident that kept him standing where he was.

On the other side of the road, a family of Mexicans stood close together. They were removed from the scene but observing carefully. Duke figured they had been in the back of the pickup— illegal aliens hitching a ride from a stranger. They didn't look hurt, though. Maybe they had caused it? So far from the border, this didn't make much sense, but sometimes wetbacks caused accidents by dashing across the road. He'd seen it before, and he'd always been moved by their bravery.

The father was dressed in a shabbier version of the same outfit Duke was wearing: a pale green golf shirt that had seen too many summers, worn and graying chinos, and a trucker's cap that

141

was nearly brand-new. The mother and daughter wore homemade dresses. From a pattern cut from a magazine, Duke imagined. The way his own mother had made dresses.

But there was something else that prevented him from returning to his car, something beyond the quaintness of this small Mexican family. Besides their obvious poverty, they had a mysterious warmth that everyone else at the scene lacked. They were bright where everyone else was dull. They were *vibrante*. They must have been worried that the Highway Patrol would soon arrive, but the intensity of their attention was even better than that.

The little girl, particularly, had a way of attending the world that made Duke want to cry. She had bright, playful eyes, but she was watching the accident with such fierce attention that Duke would have done anything to distract her. Her father's hand was in the small of her back, and Duke envied her father the calm way he kept his family in one place in what must have been extreme circumstances.

Before he realized he was going to speak to them, Duke had already passed the crowd of sturdy men and caught the eye of the older man, who was still arguing over the hood of his huge Impala. The older man stopped yelling about the damage to his car and just stared. The onlookers expanded and then contracted around the idea that John Wayne was just then walking past them.

When Duke arrived on the other side of the road, the Mexican looked up at him with neither comprehension nor dismay.

"*¿Venías en . . . la troca?*" Duke fanned his hand in the direction of the pickup.

"*Sí, señor.*"

"*¿Están bien?*"

"*Sí. Gracias.*"

"*Tu niña es muy bonita. ¿Puedo hablarle?*"

"Gracias. ¡Ándele!"

Duke bent down and smiled at the little girl. He took her hand and pointed it toward the accident. *"¿Qué estás viendo, bonita? ¿Qué es lo que ves por allá?"*

She checked her father to make sure it was all right to speak. He nodded and smiled and pushed her forward a little toward Duke. She spoke very clearly, but in the same lower-class singsong that reminded Duke of Ernesto.

"Esos hombres tan estúpidos," she said.

Duke laughed. They *were* stupid men. She was more honest than he would have been. He returned his attention to her father. *"¿Los puedo llevar a algún lado? La policía . . . la policía muy pronto."* Duke looked up the road toward his own car.

The man stared at Duke for what felt like a long time. His wife spoke to him and he spoke back, but it wasn't clear to Duke what they said. Their voices were too quick and musical for him. He wished Ernesto were here to help him. Or his daughter. Or his wife. He could feel the attention of the gringos gathering at his back. He knew that sooner or later he would have to turn around and face them.

The Mexican asked his wife another question, and then he spoke slowly in English to Duke.

"You are Mr. John Wayne?"

"Yes, I am, and I'd be happy if I could help you."

The Mexican nodded and gathered his family around him. Duke turned and walked through the staring crowd back toward his car.

As he started north, the tiny Mexican family in tow, he felt an energy in his legs and arms that he thought he'd lost forever. It was like the energy he felt some days before his cancer operation, when the world was young and he didn't have to think so much about himself. The people in their cars were watching him now with the playfulness of *hijos*. Their smiles were wide and seductive. Their eyes were bright. He wasn't a stranger to any of them, and they were happy to be seeing him on the earth after so many years of seeing him on the screen. Men who had been standing beside their cars stretched forward to shake his hand, and it occurred to him that maybe they thought he'd solved some problem down the road which they would soon hear news of. He turned around once to smile at his Mexican family. He turned around again to see if the cars had started moving, which they hadn't. He considered for a long moment all that he was walking away from.

He'd made *Sands of Iwo Jima* at Pendleton, down the road. It was a very good movie in which he'd died before the end. A ways farther down the road, he could have stopped by the Scripps Clinic, where they'd diagnosed his cancer, where he'd been forced to begin over. For a moment, he felt as large and swollen with significance as he'd ever felt in his life. He figured he had another ten years to live if he was very lucky, and he wondered if the rest of it could be as good as this. As he looked up the road he'd just driven down, toward Newport Beach, toward Hollywood, toward the rest of America, he wanted to know if there was a way to maintain this exuberance which attacked him at the oddest moments of his life. He didn't think he was going to have to leave America after all. Because he could go north as well as south and he wouldn't be any closer to himself than he'd ever been. Himself was the thing that had run away, but himself was also the thing that had come back. He didn't need to go to Mexico; Mexico was coming to him.

He turned around to face the Mexicans. He asked the father if he could drive a car. The father said yes.

CATALINA

1977

FOR SOME GODDAMN REASON, MILTON BREN HAD AN EXTRAORDINARY AMOUNT OF INFORMATION ABOUT ERROL FLYNN. SOMETHING ABOUT THIS PARTICULAR TRIP TO CATALINA HAD ACTIVATED HIS INTEREST, AND SO WHENEVER THE CONVERSATION FLAGGED——AND THIS WAS PARTICULARLY TRUE WHEN THEY ALL GOT LOADED——MILTON WOULD BRING UP SOME LITTLE known fact of Flynn's life. It was the oddest thing, but Duke thought he knew what Milton was up to. Milton couldn't stop thinking about an actor whom he admired while he enjoyed the lavish hospitality of an actor whom he didn't.

Pointing off the stern of the *Wild Goose*—Duke's 136-foot converted minesweeper—Milton went on. Pilar, Duke's wife, hung on every word. "He used to moor the *Sirocco* in that cove over there, and they'd set up a canopy on the beach for their parties. Errol liked to walk on hot coals and have all sorts of wild contests—things he'd learned how to do when he was a youngster in Tasmania. People say they were orgies, but if they were, the only one who ever got anything was Flynn. Compared to him, the rest of his friends were practically eunuchs."

Duke's head was too full of Flynn facts, and he steadied himself on the railing as he walked toward the bow. Claire had already gone to sleep, so there was no one left to talk with but Pilar and Milton. Okay, that was okay, he tried to convince himself, but he nearly fell into a deck chair, his brain was so full of horseshit and tequila. He wasn't supposed to be alone on his own ship unless he wanted to be. He stared at the island in hopes that something there might interest his eyes and therefore shut off his brain. Catalina before him was like a cluster of perfectly shaped breasts. The blue hills were calm as the sea beneath them, and the sky was black like harsh coffee with bits of bright star poking through it. Duke thought about coffee because he couldn't bear to think about breasts. A breast would make him sick, but coffee made him comfortable. Black coffee in the morning was like drinking from the core of the earth, like sustaining yourself with the deepest secret that God could keep from man.

Surrendering to his fatigue and drunkenness, he decided to sit down in the deck chair that had nearly tripped him. He remembered what Orson Welles had said about Pappy Ford. "John Ford knows what the earth is made of." What a beautiful thing to say, Duke thought, but thinking it distracted him from sitting down and he missed the chair, clipping the arm and bringing it down sideways with him onto the deck. Even as he began to understand that he was falling, he could still wish that someone had spoken so beautifully about himself.

Actually, the deck was sort of comfortable. He watched the island sideways as it gently rose and fell above his new vertical horizon. He made his right arm into a pillow and lay there for what seemed like a long time. The breasts were now upright, like a woman standing, and the sky was like a thick black curtain—embroidered with stars—that she was drawing toward her body. He had been lucky, he knew, in that the most beautiful women he could imagine *always* became his wife. He wondered now if he could marry an island.

He had to get up and pee.

He pushed himself up from the deck and set the deck chair straight before he sat down in it. Now that he was upright again, the hills no longer looked like breasts but like circus tents, and he could still hear Milton's voice, all the way around the side of the *Wild Goose,* loudly declaiming his Hollywood history lesson to Pilar, who, as a little Peruvian girl, had loved Errol Flynn and was rapt with Milton's stories. "They had mock sea battles," Milton said. "Can you fucking believe that?" For his part, Duke could imagine what a pretty boat the *Sirocco* must have been. For all his drunkenness and arrogance, Flynn had been a real sailor, the way Ford had been a real sailor, the way Duke was just a big boy from the desert who loved the sea more than anything, and that was different from being a sailor. The *Wild Goose* would never be a sailboat. The *Wild Goose* was a converted minesweeper.

God, he *really* had to pee.

Milton said, "Around the campfire, he'd tell long, complicated stories about being in the slave trade when he was a kid in New Guinea. Can you beat that? They didn't call it slavery, but then, they never do. He would rent whole tribes from their chieftains, and then sell the lease to another tribe. Sounds like he was preparing himself for the movies, doesn't it? Sounds like he was preparing himself to become a movie star."

A movie star? What the fuck did Milton know about being a movie star? Duke wished that Errol Flynn were here so that they could both tell Milton about being a movie star. Duke didn't mind signing autographs, he didn't mind being watched and photographed—in fact, he *loved* that part—but he minded being analyzed as though he were dead. He tried to be reasonable about his public statements, he tried to contribute to the nation, but there were times when he just wanted to stir things up, to release a torrent of vital energy that wasn't meant to change things so much as to remind everyone that Duke Wayne was still alive.

He stood up and sat down again. There was a deliciousness about his full bladder that he hadn't accounted for until he started taking steps to relieve it. He wanted to sit here and think for just another full moment before he visited the head. He wanted to follow one more thought down into his boozy nighttime consciousness. There was something there, and he wouldn't be able to get after it if he walked away from this spot or allowed anything to leave his body.

He shifted his ass along the chair and that relieved some of the pressure; maybe he didn't have to pee as badly as he thought.

When was the first time he realized that he had failed? It was after Ward Bond had died, when the whole world was painted with his grief. Duke had finished directing *The Alamo,* and he was waiting for the first industry reviews when he read what John Ford had said about the movie. Ford, in a fancy bit of public opinion fucking, said that it was "the most important motion picture ever made." What was he trying to do? Duke wondered as the sky grew a shade blacker with some dense clouds that had wandered in from L.A. Was he trying to hurt me in some obscure way that only an asshole like Ford could understand? The movie hadn't been anywhere near as good as that—he felt like a fucking genius because he'd been able to finish it at all—and it would have been nicer of the old man to just say as much, to say, for example, "John Wayne is a first-rate director and I'm proud to have worked with him." Or: "Wayne has done a better job of capturing the Western experience than all but a handful of men." And then he wouldn't have been left to wonder *how much* Ford was lying, which was what he was wondering right now. He had wanted to speak some great truth about the nation, but he had failed. Ford made movies that spoke the truth about the nation as an aside.

"Someone just saw a picture of him, I guess," Milton continued. "That's right. I think it was some documentary about New Guinea, and Flynn was the brave jungle guide. He did a few plays in London, but it didn't take long for Hollywood to scoop him up. He probably still had his tan from New Guinea when he did *Captain Blood.*"

What the *fuck* did he know about it? Duke thought. There was so much work between being a young man and being an old man, so many years of pissing yourself away and not knowing what for, and then one day they wake you up to tell you you're a star, and you *still* feel like you pissed away so much of yourself getting there. Work and success were *not* connected as far as he could tell. Work was what he did to distract himself while other, more painful processes took place within him. Because the work was always either horrible or wonderful and had nothing to do with how much he was getting paid or how many people were watching him. It made him wonder about the pressure that a great man like Ford must have been under. He still wanted to know what Ford was thinking when he said those words. Ford's feelings for him had always been equal parts hatred and love, but Duke didn't mind the hatred because there was *so much love.* Of course, Duke thanked him at the time—there was nothing to do but thank him—yet there was still so much he didn't understand. Maybe there was less to understand than he thought. Pappy Ford's head was full of hell. But he behaved better than any man Duke knew who was half as wretched.

When it was all over, when everyone he knew was as dead as Ward Bond and John Ford, what would any of them get credit for? He'd grown so accustomed to this view of Catalina, after all his trips to this little bay beside the isthmus, that he probably didn't see it anymore unless he was stumbling drunk or driven to poetic distraction by Milton's inane ramblings. Maybe this moment was the only one he would ever get points for: holding his piss long enough to spend a few extra minutes staring at a beautiful island.

He shifted in his chair again, but this time it did no good—the pressure against his bladder was painful and he would not be able to resist much longer.

What was he looking at anyway? He could no longer hear Milton, and he hoped this meant he had decided to kill himself and spare Duke any more bullshit for the rest of the trip. He was looking at three now-cloudless hills, which seemed to him the essence of all that was beautiful about his Southern California. They reminded him of their sisters, the Coast Ranges on the other side of the channel, and they were radiantly brown. How could something be "radiantly brown"? His first wife's hair had been "radiantly brown." His youngest son's skin in the summertime was "radiantly brown." The sunset, tinted by the smog, could sometimes be "radiantly brown." Words that didn't belong together were always together. Right now, for example, his need to urinate was "pleasantly painful." He was "morbidly enthusiastic" about the rest of his life.

He thought hard about this. Maybe everything that *seemed* divided was really connected, not just words but EVERYTHING. These hills were connected under the channel to the hills near his home. The water that rocked him now was the same water that had rocked him forty years ago when he spent his first weekend on John Ford's sailboat. The hills were one with the hills. The water was one with the water. And his own life, which seemed so divided from everyone else's, was really just a version of the same big life, the same big earth, the same big sea. Maybe that's what Orson Welles meant when he was talking about Ford. Maybe Ford knew this. Maybe that's what Ford meant when he was talking about Wayne. There wasn't one film, there was all film. There wasn't one man, there were all men. As he continued to stare at the island, he started to get a boner, which rose and illuminated his whole body until he could feel himself radiantly brown, too. Maybe he *could* fuck an island? Maybe he had reached a point in his career where anything was possible. He wanted to believe it—God, he wanted to believe it. He closed his eyes and opened them again. The hills were still there: radiant, alluring, vulnerable, wanting him. In the foreground, there were only a few other boats attending the hills, and they seemed almost religious in the way they didn't crowd or dismay the island itself. Above, the sky was thicker with stars than Duke had ever seen it.

His moment had arrived. If God was watching, Duke was certain that this was the moment of his election. Whatever shitty things he had done in his life, he had been forgiven them for the virtue of this single perception. The island was beautiful and he saw it as beautiful. Maybe for this moment, and in this exact way, he was the only person who saw it. The dark radiance of the hills was now his radiance, too. He stood up from the chair and began to walk carefully toward the head.

His muscles ached and he still really had to pee, but he felt happy and completed.

As he followed the curve of the bulkhead, he began to hear Milton again. Some miracle of acoustics and water and ship's metal had baffled the sound long enough for Duke to have his moment of redemption. He was going to heaven after all, and soon he would have the empty bladder of an angel. He was grateful to Milton for driving him into the wilderness of his own boat, and he resolved that he would give him a gift when he got the chance. Milton also seemed to have reached some final chapter of his story.

"And for a while he just sailed off the coast of Spain—or between Portugal and Spain, maybe—and thought about how much he'd like to pay off his back taxes, and thought about how much he missed his friends, and tried to swim more and drink less and give his buckshot liver time to resurrect itself, but I think he knew in his heart that the great party he'd had was almost over, that most of what he'd loved and lived for was in some other part of the world which he would never see again. I think he must have been pretty resigned to it, or at least that's the way it seems from the writing he did at the time. I think he must have been, in his own Errol Flynnish way, happy."

He could hear Pilar chirp and laugh and clap her hands. She wouldn't fake enthusiasm over such things, and so Duke had to believe she had enjoyed the story. In his heart, he was glad she'd been entertained.

Pilar laughed until she saw Duke lumbering up the passage-way toward them. Milton flipped his cigarette into the water and smiled like a man who probably never had to pee this badly in his life, like a man who didn't have the *cojones* to drink that deeply of his experience. Oh hell, Duke thought, someday he'll have his moment, too. That's why he couldn't stop talking about Flynn—he admired the kind of life he wasn't capable of living. Milton was sad because he hadn't yet sat in the darkness and watched an island fill with the radiance of God's grace. Duke's bladder was as big as the world. His own *cojones* were heavy enough to break buildings. He gently nudged Pilar aside before he unzipped his trousers and relieved himself entirely on Milton's blue deck shoes.

Duke loved the world, and the world loved Duke. Milton Bren didn't say another word about Errol Flynn for the rest of the trip.

THEY WERE EXPENDABLE

1979

THE BOY IN TRACTION ON THE NEXT BED WAS DRINKING WINE FROM A PAPER CUP. HIS OLDER BROTHER WAS POURING MORE. THEY'D BEEN IN A MOTORCYCLE ACCIDENT TOGETHER, AND ALTHOUGH THE OLDER BROTHER HADN'T REQUIRED HOSPITALIZATION, A DRAMATICALLY FRESH SCAR STRETCHED ACROSS HIS JAW.

DANNY BARDEN HEARD

the door open as he watched the wine bottle and the paper cups disappear. Everything was swallowed by a blue backpack that the older brother carefully lowered to the floor. It was Sister Anthony. Of all the nurses and nuns who strolled through his room, she was the most likely to guess what had been hidden from her. In her early forties, stout like a former athlete, she watched the world with informed disapproval, as though she could see what was wrong but was too amused to bother correcting anyone.

"What's going on here? I don't trust young men when they're quiet." She adjusted Danny's bed and took his pulse. She smiled at the motorcycle boys with affection that Danny could feel.

"Your mother called," she said to him. "She'll be here before dinner. If you want anything, I'm to call her. Your mother's a wonderful woman. I'd do anything for her."

It felt like a reproach. Danny scratched at the stubble on his face and pushed his long hair away from his forehead. "She just acts that way," he said, "because she's still afraid of nuns."

Sister Anthony smiled and stuck a thermometer in his mouth. "You'll be able to take more medication soon," she said. He didn't feel pain so much as a loud numbness. He knew what pain was from yesterday.

Danny had fluid around his testicles. "Hydrocele" was what they called it. Yesterday morning, they had cut open his scrotum. He thought he could feel the wound still draining, and as the drugs began to wear off, his groin burned. He had drifted in and out of being too numb to feel anything. There was Demerol to ease the pain and Valium to calm him down.

Sister Anthony wanted to tell him something. She tucked away the simple gold crucifix that had been bouncing against her brown sweater as she worked. She touched Danny's clock radio, which was at that moment playing a Jackson Browne song that Danny should have recognized.

"What?" Danny mumbled. "What?"

She looked him over. She removed the thermometer, read it, and then shook it hard.

"You wanted to tell me something," Danny said. "I can read your mind."

The radio segued from the song into a news report. Sister Anthony turned it up. "John Wayne, who entered UCLA Medical Center last month, has begun a series of experimental interferon treatments. Wayne's family has made no comment on this latest round in his battle against cancer."

Sister Anthony leaned toward Danny and whispered, "I don't want to upset the younger boys. This is only for you. But I've got this feeling that John Wayne is going to die tonight."

"What makes you think that?"

"Oh, it's just the way they're talking about him. Everyone knows something that no one wants to say."

"What don't they want to say?"

"You know. That a man like that could die."

She tossed her hands dismissively as if she couldn't bear to say it, either. Something buried deep was about to surface. Would she cry? Closing her eyes and touching her mouth, she turned from Danny to adjust the traction above the motorcycle boy's bed.

Danny couldn't muster much feeling for John Wayne right now. He wondered if there was something wrong with him. When his Uncle Jimmy had died of a heroin overdose the year before, it hadn't bothered him that much, either. It had been coming for a long time and he'd become used to the idea. When his father told him, it seemed like something he already knew.

Thinking about his father, Danny felt guilty. His father didn't know he was in the hospital. His father didn't even know he was in Southern California. Somehow, in the planning for this operation, he'd been left out. *Danny knew what it was.* Telling his father would have guaranteed a scene. Two years divorced but still supernaturally bitter, Frank Barden would have turned the hospital room into a battlefield. Danny's mother had said, "Just don't tell him. I'd really appreciate it if you didn't tell him."

Danny missed his father, though. It was a strange thing how he could miss his father. Even when he didn't speak to him for months, he needed to have objects around him that reminded him of Frank Barden. The clock radio, for instance, was from his father's cabinet shop. As an idea, his father sustained himself against all odds. In moments of candor made possible by large amounts of beer, Danny wondered if Frank Barden wasn't just a character he had invented so that he could have a really sad story to tell himself. *My father doesn't love me* was how the story went.

He tried to imagine what his father was doing now, just ten miles away from Saint Joseph's Hospital. He must be at the cabinet shop, keeping busy. It was a soft, overcast early summer day, and with the huge loading doors opened onto the lumberyard, his work would seem as much outside as in. John Wayne was at UCLA—this wasn't like his last trip to Hoag Memorial. If Duke were still in Orange County, there would be less to worry about. UCLA was where famous rich people went *to die.* His father was working hard, Danny could feel it. Frank Barden was wearing his glasses near the end of his nose, staring down at beautiful pieces of wood that would become cabinets in his thick hands.

Danny heard the door close as Sister Anthony left the room. The motorcycle boys cautiously returned to the party, which she had interrupted. They now shared one cup of wine between them.

He remembered their names. Paul was the boy in traction and Jake was his older brother.

"Does she think I'm going to start crying about John Wayne?" Paul asked.

Jake shrugged.

"I think I sold drugs to his son once," Paul added.

"What do you mean? You don't know who you were selling drugs to?"

"Someone told me later that this guy was John Wayne's son. I don't know whether it was true or not."

"You probably shouldn't say it, then. I feel sorry for these guys that have famous fathers."

"That's cool."

Jake was almost as big as Danny, and the scar across his jaw gave him a pleasantly dangerous look. Danny had heard that Jake worked at an RV factory. His broad shoulders confirmed that. He had the scarred hands of a journeyman carpenter. He probably spent his days putting together huge vehicles from prefabricated panels, but he was on his way to some real skills if his heart was in it. Danny wanted to tell Jake that his father had remodeled John Wayne's house, that he was a master carpenter and a successful contractor, that Danny himself had spent years in the cabinet shop and on job sites scarring his own hands and building his own shoulders. He also wanted to tell him that he'd rode dirt bikes with the son whom Jake was defending. He wanted to tell him, but he didn't know how to tell him.

Jake noticed Danny's interest in the conversation. "Hey, where did you say you were going to college?"

"Berkeley," Danny said.

"Hell," Jake said. "Why'd you go so far away from home? Why didn't you go to UCLA or UCI or someplace around here?"

"I don't know," Danny said. "It was where I wanted to go." He didn't mean to sound sullen, but suddenly it was hard to explain himself. To their credit, Jake and Paul didn't seem to take it personally.

"That's cool," Paul said. "I know what you mean."

He'd gone to Berkeley because it was the best school he could get into. One of his father's associates—maybe Michael Wayne—had called it "the little red schoolhouse." That was supposed to be an anti-communist remark, but it sounded more anti-intellectual to Danny. His father and the men who informed his opinions would have preferred USC, a school that would have prepared him for a career rather than just more school.

In the forty-five minutes it took his mother to arrive at the hospital, the dull pressure in Danny's groin became a sharp pain. The drugs had worn off. Everything in the room became more pointed and clear to him. He listened carefully as his father's clock radio flipped its numbers, and the clicking sound was more important to him than the music. Time was tangible—each moment a little metal card that flipped over to reveal the next moment. At 5:47 P.M., Lillian opened the door. It seemed to him that her authority emptied the room of everything but itself. Even the chairs and the medical instruments were changed by her presence. Jake and Paul turned to watch her. She smiled at them until they smiled back.

Lillian kissed Danny and pushed his long hair away from his forehead. "That Sister Anthony is a pistol," she said. "I was watching her fill the little cups with pills, and she said, 'This one's to relieve his pain, and this one's to relieve his sarcasm.' "

Danny smiled in spite of his desire to stay beyond his mother's reach.

"Have you been giving the nuns a hard time?" Lillian asked.

"I was born to give the nuns a hard time."

Now it was Lillian's turn to smile, in spite of her wish to remain safe from his new tone.

"Sister Anthony told me something really strange," Lillian said.

"She thinks John Wayne's going to die tonight," Danny said.

"Yeah, and when she said it, I thought, Maybe she's right. I've been sad all day, and I don't know why."

Danny pulled himself up higher in the bed. The pain in his testicles expanded through his pelvis and thighs. A quick but terrible nausea blinked through his stomach.

"You okay, sweetheart?"

"I'm praying to Saint Joseph for more drugs."

Lillian stepped toward the door and spoke to someone in the hall. When she returned, she held Danny's hand.

"Did she look like she was on her way in here?"

"Yes, honey. She said she'd be here in just a minute. Hang on, okay?" Lillian held his hand tighter, and Danny was surprised by how much that helped.

Lillian sat in the chair beside Danny's bed. She wore that vacant look Danny had always hated. Her eyes were moist.

"Mom?"

She turned toward him. Her eyes focused. "He was such a big part of our lives."

"He's not going to die tonight," Danny said. "You're just freaked out by these nuns."

The door opened, but Sister Anthony didn't appear. Instead, a younger nun with pale skin and large breasts brought a Dixie cup to Danny's bedside. At first, Danny couldn't guess her mission, he had prepared himself so well for Sister Anthony to deliver him from pain. The young woman announced herself as Sister Margaret and poured him a cup of water. She had blond hair and a small straight nose. As he swallowed the pills, Danny wanted to tell her she was too pretty to be a nun.

"Where's Sister Anthony?" Lillian asked.

"She got called away for a moment." And then, as if that didn't explain enough, "She's pretty upset."

Lillian and Danny looked at each other.

"What's she upset about?" Danny asked.

Sister Margaret hesitated. Danny watched her eyes cloud with self-counsel. Jake turned from his brother's bed, and Sister Margaret became aware that she had an audience. "He's seen a priest," she finally said.

"Who?" Jake asked.

"She's talking about John Wayne," Danny said.

"He isn't a Catholic, is he?" Lillian asked Danny.

"No," Danny said. "But all his wives and children were." He was troubled by his own interest. The Valium hadn't yet reestablished his distance from himself.

"How do you know that?" Lillian asked. "They reported this on the news?"

"Jeez," Danny said.

"What?" Lillian asked.

"He's chickening out. I can't believe it."

"I didn't think he was a hero of yours."

"He isn't, but I didn't think he'd become a fucking Catholic."

Sister Margaret's eyes narrowed and she looked down toward the bed. He'd forgotten that she was a nun. He wanted to apologize, but before he could, she'd walked away from his bed and out of the room. Jake smiled and turned back toward his brother, who seemed to have fallen asleep.

Danny was ashamed of himself. He'd stepped over his new ironic detachment into callousness.

"Honey, maybe you should try to sleep."

Danny didn't want to sleep. Shame had brought him back to his father. It was early evening and Frank Barden would still be working in the shop. Since he'd quit drinking, he often spent evenings alone, working on cabinets he didn't need to finish for weeks. Danny could see his father now as clearly as if he were standing in the room. He'd lost a lot of weight from sobriety and divorce. His hair was now frizzy gray. Danny could see Frank's sawdust-spotted overalls. He could see his strong but trembling hands.

Danny could never work in the shop alone. For all the time he'd spent assisting his father, he'd never learned the skills to build a cabinet by himself. He heard Jake laughing with his brother and he envied him what Frank Barden hadn't offered either of his own sons. These days, as Chris wore the same overalls Danny had worn two years ago, he encountered the same resistance. Danny's father always said that there would be time, that it was more important to learn basics than the big picture. He'd been pulling the same shit on Chris since Danny left for college. They had learned how to saw, but not how to measure; how to attach laminate, but not how to draw plans; how to finish, but not how to begin. In terms of carpentry, it was an enforced infancy. Maybe his father was afraid that if he passed on too many skills, his boys would never return to him. Maybe he was right.

Lillian stood by the window and watched Orange County. Danny studied her back. She had broad shoulders and a narrow torso—she seemed too skinny from this angle. Danny worried about his mother, and he wanted to know how she could be sad about John Wayne. She had so many other things to be sad about.

"Tell me something," Lillian said. She'd made it from the window to the bedside without Danny noticing the transition. "Was I being selfish to not tell your father about this? Would you feel better if your father was here?"

Danny couldn't imagine where she'd found such a thought. It scared him. How could she be so uncertain about such a basic understanding between them? It reminded him of how many times she had promised to divorce his father before she finally came through.

"I keep thinking he must be in a lot of pain," she said.

"Why do you think that?"

"Alice makes it sound like he's so lonely, and I can't help thinking about that apartment Chris says he's living in. It sounds awful."

This didn't seem like his mother, but he thought he understood. John Wayne was dying, and it was a good day to feel sorry for Frank Barden. "I don't know what you're talking about," Danny said.

"I'm talking about I'm not sure I made the right decision, that's all." In a few seconds, she had become a different woman—a woman who couldn't defend herself, a woman who needed him.

"It was *our* decision," Danny said.

Her skin drew tightly over her cheekbones. For a moment, she didn't look like anyone else in his family.

"It's too late anyway," Danny said. He didn't know what he meant by that, but his mother did. Her face softened.

"I guess you're right," she said. "It's probably not the best time to tell him, after the operation's over."

The nuns returned to the room. Their eyes were bright and powerful, as though they were grateful to be alive or afraid of death or about to cause harm to someone they loved. They watched

164

Danny and they watched Paul. Sister Anthony looked better than Danny had ever seen her—as though she'd borrowed some of the younger nun's beauty.

It was almost six o'clock and the news would soon be on. Danny imagined that their behavior had something to do with that. There was a TV in the common room next door, and he wondered why they weren't waiting there. His own radio had been playing softly, but Danny hardly noticed it anymore. He reached over to turn it up in the middle of a slow Springsteen song that Jake seemed to recognize. He tapped the side of his brother's bed, closed his eyes, and whispered the lyrics. Lillian, who had taken a seat beside Danny's bed, asked if there was anything he wanted.

Danny ignored her. "Jake?"

Jake opened his eyes. "Yeah?"

"We didn't tell you before," Danny said, "but we knew John Wayne. My dad remodeled that house in Newport Beach."

"That's wild," Jake said.

"It's not a big secret," Danny said. "We just don't talk about it as much as we used to. We used to talk about it all the time."

Lillian tried to smile. Her effort lacked enthusiasm.

"You must be bummed," Jake said.

"My mom is."

Lillian completely lost her smile. The nuns, who had been watching Danny, stepped toward the end of the bed.

"His father built that house in Newport Beach," Jake said.

"What house?" Sister Anthony asked.

"John Wayne's house."

The nuns changed. Danny could feel their spirits surging toward him over the end of the bed.

"They built some apartment buildings together, too," Danny said.

"What's he like?" Sister Margaret asked. "Does he seem like a man who can admit when he's been wrong?"

Danny was perplexed by Sister Margaret's question.

"He's a nice man," Lillian said. "Very respectful of other people, especially women."

"That's good," Sister Anthony said. "That will help."

"Help what?" Jake asked.

"Maybe it sounds crazy," Sister Anthony said, "but I find that people who've been gentle with others during their lives can be gentle with themselves when they're dying."

"Oh, I thought you were going to say that God would go easy on him."

"Well, maybe that, too," Sister Margaret said.

"You know," Sister Anthony said, "I remember the greatest John Wayne movie. I saw it when I was a little girl. It was so sad. It was about PT boats in the Philippines. For some reason, I can't get it out my head. What was it called?"

"They Were Expendable," Danny said.

"Yes, that was it. Donna Reed was in it. And Robert Montgomery. It was just so sad. Donna Reed and John Wayne were falling in love, but everything was coming down around them. We were retreating from the Philippines at the start of the war, and he had to leave her there. I fell in love with him because he did his duty. Oh, it was just so awfully sad."

For a moment, everyone considered Sister Anthony's movie. Danny remembered it perfectly because he'd seen it the year before at the Pacific Film Archive. It was a movie about defeat, and she was right—it was one of the saddest movies he'd ever seen. Donna Reed was a nurse. Robert Montgomery wore shorts. John Wayne wore a baseball cap. Finally, Jake broke the silence.

"I'm not sure he was such a great guy," he said.

"What do you mean?" Lillian asked.

"I don't know. I heard stories in Newport Beach about things that would happen."

"What kinds of things?" Sister Margaret wanted to know.

"A friend of mine was swimming in the bay once, and she got really tired. She tried to climb up on his dock, but he wouldn't help her."

"He was standing there?" Sister Margaret asked.

"Yeah, he was just standing there, yelling at her to get off his dock."

"That doesn't sound right," Sister Anthony said. "Maybe he was afraid she was trespassing."

"She was *drowning,*" Jake said.

Everyone kept silent. The nuns had reached the end of their desire to argue with Jake. Lillian and Danny, who had special knowledge of John Wayne, couldn't speak about what they knew without speaking about Frank Barden. Where *is* your father? Danny wanted someone to ask. He wanted someone to ask so that he could tell them, *My father's alone.*

"Maybe he was drunk?" Danny suggested.

"I've seen him drunk," Jake said.

"You have?"

"I ate dinner next to him once."

"When was this?" Paul spoke from behind him. Danny had forgotten he was there.

"When Judy's parents took us to The Chart House."

"What was he like?" Danny asked.

"He was all right," Jake admitted. "But I could tell that he was a complicated guy. He got a little tweaked. It was weird."

"What happened?" Danny asked.

"He just got mad at things that weren't any big deal, like they didn't have the kind of hot sauce he liked, but then later he apologized, and I'm pretty sure he left a big tip."

"I don't think you can talk about a man based on just a few things you know," Lillian said. "There are always lots of other things."

It irritated Danny that she could talk this way. "What do you mean?"

"It doesn't feel right to pass judgment on him based on just a few things that happened. Or on his movies. Or on anything. I don't think we should be that way." Lillian was sticking up for herself, but she was also sticking up for Frank. At the bottom of her list, she was sticking up for John Wayne.

"I'm just telling you what I saw," Jake said.

Lillian moved toward the window. The nuns drifted out the door. There were still a couple of minutes before the six o'clock news. As the clock radio continued to play soft folky music, Lillian stared through the window at flat and smoggy Orange County. Danny watched her back and remembered how Satan had taken Christ to the top of a tower and offered him all the kingdoms of the world. His mother was planning to move to San Francisco. She was going to give Chris the choice of going to high school in Orange County or coming along. The whole thing was so reasonable, but Danny couldn't help thinking that this was the sin which would gain her the whole world. For Chris, it wasn't really a choice. He was a good Catholic boy, and he would follow his martyred father. Lillian would be free. Maybe she was thinking about her freedom right now? She couldn't be responsible any longer, Danny could hear her think. The ruin of her marriage was not her fault, had never been her fault. When would it end? When would she get to live her own life? She needed a new kingdom or she would throw herself off the tower and there would be no angels below to catch her.

Lately, he'd begun to hate her for how much she didn't understand the significance of her own life. Right now, she was just a skinny woman standing before a gray window, but she was also a larger person than anyone he'd ever known. Her life had been more terrifying and heroic than any he'd read about. Why couldn't she see herself?

So quickly that on another day it would have killed him, Danny realized how much he loved her. He loved the way she lied to herself, and he loved the way she caught herself in her own lies. He loved the way she could be stronger than anyone he knew, and yet break when anyone else would have held. She dared him to become a great man without guessing what that might lead to, and she happily offered him the tools to leave home while she resented every step he took away from her. As the glossy suburban light gathered around her figure in the window, he had to admit that he also loved her for being beautiful. She was a pretty mother to have even when her heart was harder than any man's.

When Lillian finally turned around to face him, it was because Sister Anthony had returned to the room. She was more harried than the last time. She no longer wore her brown sweater. Her crucifix bounced against her chest. She was so white that she glowed.

"They've given him *extreme unction.*"

Danny knew what the words meant, but it surprised him that the nun hadn't thought to explain.

"Is he dead?" Lillian asked.

"We don't know that," Sister Anthony said. "We don't know anything about that." Her face was flushed. She was happy. "He's become a Catholic. He's been baptized."

Danny accepted her enthusiasm as well as he could, but it was difficult not to be scared. John Wayne had become a Catholic. Why was that such a terrifying idea?

Danny had seen Sister Anthony's movie and many more. In the last two years, he'd seen more John Wayne movies than anyone he knew. It seemed as though the further away from Frank Barden his life took him, the more he wanted to understand John Wayne. In this project, he'd given up his irony a long time ago.

Danny had spent his whole life trying to remain safe from the drama—the drama of his parents, the drama of John Wayne. He wanted everyone to know how much he'd tried to remain safe. He found the button for his bed and raised himself so that he could see what his mother had been looking at through the window. He wanted to see what she thought she was leaving, what he had already left. The machinery clicked and whirred until his torso was almost perpendicular to his legs. His testicles pained him, but the burning sensation had been replaced by an oddly reassuring *itch*. He needed to pee, and for the first time since his operation, he was looking forward to the process of getting from the bed to the bathroom.

He looked over to ask for help and he saw his mother holding Sister Anthony. He couldn't say what had happened in the minute he'd been looking away from them, but it must have been something good. Lillian was staring at him over Sister Anthony's shoulder, a smile that he couldn't account for just breaking her lips. Sister Anthony began to sob without remorse—she was seizing air and letting it go in painful chirps, her head beating slowly against

Lillian's shoulder. Danny would wait a moment before he interrupted them. He would wait until the nun stopped crying.

It was time for the six o'clock news. His radio chimed the change of program. He could feel that an announcement would be made. But John Wayne wasn't dead yet—Danny knew that. John Wayne was alive somewhere in Southern California. And so was Frank Barden. But soon they would both be dead.

Sister Anthony retreated a step from Lillian. Danny closed his eyes so that he could see his father. He could smell his skin and see his eyes fill with watery light. Frank Barden was drunk or crying or both. He was missing John Wayne and he was missing Lillian.

IN HARM'S
WAY

1979

ACCORDING TO DUKE'S SON MICHAEL, HANK FONDA HAD SAID, "WELL THEN, I'LL JUST SIT HERE UNTIL HE *DOES* HAVE TIME TO SEE ME." MICHAEL'S INTENTION TO KEEP FONDA AWAY FROM HIS FATHER CRUMBLED ALMOST AT ONCE. BUT HE STILL MADE FONDA WAIT ALMOST AN HOUR BEFORE HE WOULD LET HIM INTO THE ICU.

ONCE THERE, FONDA DIStinguished himself by not reacting at all to the carnage that was spread before him—John Wayne's own body as ropey and frail as famine, his movements difficult to comprehend but certainly painful, his eyes wide with the remoteness of suppressed terror. Sinatra had been let through the door a day earlier, and he couldn't take it. He bent over as though he was going to puke all over the nurse's cart. He held his wife for support. Fonda, who brought no wife nor needed any support, looked at Duke the way he'd looked across the fourth wall of many movies—an unhurried but voracious glance, open like a net thrown over a school of fish. Fonda said, "I'm sorry to see you feeling so bad." He held Duke's hand across the bar that kept him from rolling out of bed. "I came to say that I'll do anything I can to help you."

"You got past Michael," Duke said. "That was quite an accomplishment. He's been pissing off a lot of people."

"He's still a kid." Fonda smiled. "He's easily impressed by dedication and nerve."

Duke smiled, too. He knew what Hank meant.

"I would have never done it," Duke said. "But I'm glad that someone I know did."

Fonda smiled his longest smile. "Done what?" he quietly asked. "What are we talking about?"

"I would have never hit Ford. But I'm glad somebody I know did it. I'm even glad it was you."

"I never hit Jack." Fonda kept up his smile. "Did Jack tell you that?"

Fonda finally sat down. He approached the task carefully, like an old man. His hands were harsh and cramped as he pulled lightly at the bar. Duke could see the specter of Fonda's own death in his weathered hands.

Relaxing, Fonda said, "No, I didn't do any such thing. He

hit *me,* and then I looked back up at him—he knocked me *down*—and I thought, This is like punching your mother in the stomach, this is like breaking your father's arms. I couldn't do it. He had a way of seeming frail sometimes even when he wasn't so frail. He was an old man then, almost as old as we are now, but he wasn't *that* old. Maybe it was the booze. It had to be the booze."

"Bite your tongue," Duke whispered.

"What?" Fonda said.

"Don't say anything bad about booze to a man who's dying and hasn't had a drink in six months."

"Pardon me." Fonda dipped his head. "I thought I was talking to the still living and the still drinking."

Wayne smiled. "No, you're talking to the dead and dry."

"You really gonna die, Duke?"

"After you leave here, I'm going to call in the priest and become a Catholic."

"No shit?"

"Absolutely. Cover all the bases."

"I guess that means you're gonna die." Fonda spoke quietly.

"Yeah."

"Well, I don't want to keep you from your God. You want me to leave now?"

"No."

They talked about the obvious things first. The trips to Mexico, the difficulties with their wives, the children who were trouble to them. That took about twenty minutes. And then they were left with the only thing that was really worth talking about: the Coach.

"You really didn't hit him?" Duke asked. "For *years,* I've thought about that."

"Like I told you before"—Hank smiled—"I really didn't hit him."

175

"He hit you?"

"He hit me."

"Christ, I'm trying to picture that."

"Jesus, Duke, he was one of the meanest sons of bitches alive. Why are you having trouble picturing that?"

"This is what I'm saying—he was mean, but I don't remember him ever hitting an actor. He didn't *need* to. You must be the only actor he ever hit."

"He hit you, didn't he?"

"Oh, yeah, but that was different. That was before I was an actor. What did you do to him?"

"I was just trying to help."

"Oh, that was a great fucking idea." Duke laughed hard enough to hurt himself.

"You okay?"

"No, I'm fucking dying."

"Besides that."

"Yeah, I'm okay."

For a while, they both stared at the wall beyond Duke's bed. Amid all the machinery and hospital carts and vinyl curtains, there was one bare wall with nothing on it but dull white paint.

"You know," Duke said, "he got you that movie."

"What movie?"

"*Mister Roberts*. He told them he wouldn't direct it unless you were the star. They didn't want you to be the star."

"I was the star on Broadway."

"I know that."

"And they didn't want me?"

"They didn't want you. Ford convinced them."

"Jesus, no wonder he was mad."

"He didn't think you were being properly grateful."

"For what I didn't know about."

"Exactly."

"Jesus."

Fonda looked as though he'd lost something important. For a moment, he seemed more stricken than the patient. Duke was sorry he had mentioned it, but he was glad for his ability to surprise, even as he was dying. He had so much more that he could have told Fonda—conversations with Ford about Fonda's abilities as a leading man, a lifelong commentary on Hank's choices in women, remarks about his daughter, all manner of things that would have hurt. But there were many years when Duke might have hated Hank, and somehow never did. Hank was a brother, and hatred was immaterial when it came to brothers.

"What else have you got to tell me that will ruin my day?" Fonda asked.

"Nothing," Duke replied.

"Don't you think I have things to tell you that will ruin *your* day?"

"You won't tell me because I'm dying."

"That's right."

"But please tell me *something.*"

"Something I've never told you before?"

"That would be good."

"Okay. You were great in that Preminger picture."

"*In Harm's Way*?"

"How many other Preminger pictures were you in, Duke?"

"All right."

"Yeah, I could never get over how great you were in that movie. You were almost as good as you were with Ford and Hawks."

"Almost, huh?"

"What do you want from me? You did better than anyone. Am I going to remind you on your deathbed of all the lousy pictures you made?"

"Hell, no. Not you."

"*In Harm's Way* was a great fucking film. I was jealous of how good you were. I cried. You made me cry."

"Hey, you were in it, too."

"Just barely."

"It *was* a great picture, wasn't it?"

"Yeah."

"How many great pictures do you think we were in?"

"Oh, maybe four or five each."

"We did better than anybody, didn't we?"

"Yes, we did."

Duke smiled, and it was becoming difficult to smile. Hank smiled back to let him know that he appreciated the gesture.

"So, what's this bullshit about becoming a Catholic? You held out for so fucking long, I don't know why you're giving in now."

"Like I said, cover all the bases."

"Maybe you just think you'll have a little more juice with Ford if you make an appropriate concession before you enter the afterlife."

"Could be."

"You always were a kiss-ass, Eagle Scout, brown-nosing motherfucker, weren't you, Duke?"

"That's right."

"And I was always getting beaten up because I didn't have the courage to get down on my knees."

"There were lots of things worth fighting for, and you never had a clue what they were."

"Ah, you're probably right. And I'm old enough to admit it."

"I've lived long enough to hear Fonda admit what an asshole he is. Glory Hallelujah."

"Yes, you have. So, what are you going to do when I leave here. Call in the padre? Make a confession?"

"Worse than that," Duke said. "I'm going to get down on my knees and stick my big nose right up God's ass."

"He always loved you," Hank said. "Me, he tried to love. Never quite got the hang of it, though."

Duke smiled with the grace of the exhausted. "Who are we talking about? John Ford or Jesus Christ?"

Hank laughed.

ABOUT THE AUTHOR

DAN BARDEN grew up in Southern California and studied English literature at UC Berkeley. After several years spent running a construction company, he made his way east to earn an M.F.A. at Columbia. Barden has written for *Details* and *GQ,* and lives in New York City. This is his first novel.